No Higher Opinion

** THE DUELING SEASON IS A
SEQUENTIAL SERIES MEANT TO BE READ
IN ORDER OF PUBLICATION. **

also by shirley marks

Author's Note

Lady Frances Abbott first appeared in her sister's book *Lady Eugenia's Holiday*. *Matter of Affection* is the conclusion of her tale.
S.M.

THE DUELING SEASON
BOOK 2

No Higher Opinion

SHIRLEY MARKS

** THE DUELING SEASON IS A
SEQUENTIAL SERIES MEANT TO BE READ
IN ORDER OF PUBLICATION. **

ISBN-13: 978-1-946314-08-6 (paperback)
ISBN-10: 1-9463-1408-0

ISBN-13: 978-1-946314-09-3 (ebook)
ISBN-10: 1-946314-09-9

Anthenaeum.org
Henry Raeburn - Elizabeth Campbell portrait

www.ShirleyMarks.com

dedicated to the following ...
in chronological order

Heidi Ashworth (1996)
thank you for writing Ancilla's Story

C Lo (2006)
a family friend who inspired a hero and started
it all

Grace S (2013)
a most charming lady of my acquaintance

Dr E Robinson (2014)
who selected the status and surname of a
heroine

P Walsh (2015)
your wit and cheek,
Drayton Court Hotel, Ealing, London

Mary Beth C (2015)
we will always have Paris

Denise S (2015)
who allowed me to graft from her family tree

Nurse Hefflefinger (2016)
for her kindness and care

and finally...

Rachel and Kim for their comments,
suggestions, and time

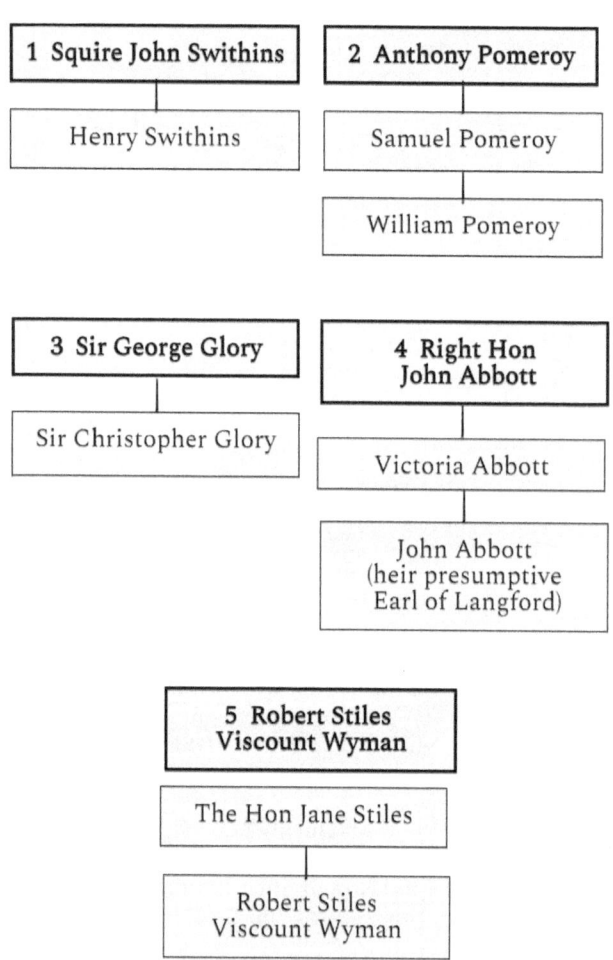

**Grace, Lady Yardley
Early Marriages**

1 Squire John Swithins

Henry Swithins

2 Anthony Pomeroy

Samuel Pomeroy

William Pomeroy

3 Sir George Glory

Sir Christopher Glory

**4 Right Hon
John Abbott**

Victoria Abbott

John Abbott
(heir presumptive
Earl of Langford)

**5 Robert Stiles
Viscount Wyman**

The Hon Jane Stiles

Robert Stiles
Viscount Wyman

No Higher Opinion

one

MAY 1812, CHALK FARMS

"Seven! Eight! Nine! Ten!"

Lord Peter Grant and Sir Milton Leech stepped the twenty paces, turned, and faced one another. After several painful, drawn out seconds, nearing a full minute's time, that was meant to increase the anticipation, merely extended the waiting period for the spectators.

No one appeared impatient, rather, they enjoyed the performance.

"Boiled!" Lord Grant exclaimed.

"Roasted!" Sir Milton shouted.

The men leveled their pistols at the other, taking aim. After several seconds more, both men raised their barrels, stretching their arms upward to a vertical position, and discharged their weapons!

The crowd applauded and cheered. The clouds of smoke rolled through the air, when it cleared the men strode to the table containing the pistol box and relinquished their weapons.

"Well done, Grant." Sir Milton congratulated his opponent.

"And you, Sir Milton, well done." Lord Grant returned the compliment. There was a round of polite applause from the on-lookers.

"Shall we be off for a bite?" Sir Milton suggested.

"What shall we have?"

"Beef, of course, and a good claret."

"I say we head off to the Club." Lord Grant clapped Sir Milton on the back.

"I will sit down to a *boiled* joint, if you don't mind."

"I will have several thick slices of *roasted* beef. No need to meet on the field over it again, what?" Lord Grant motioned for Sir Milton to lead the way. What man could be more generous than to allow one's dueling opponent to precede him?

"Right you are, Grant." Sir Milton had a hearty laugh. The participants and spectators began to clear the field within a matter of minutes.

Mr. Brathwaite had almost had enough with these fool jackanapes. Of course he was paid for his time but rising at an early hour grew tiresome. Especially since most of these things ended with the participants sharing a meal and discussing their next lark. Perhaps this could be better tolerated if they included him in the lunch invitation as well.

Given the choice, would the surgeon have preferred boiled or roasted beef?

"Good morning, Liddell." Martin Chandler entered Grayson House and removed his hat.

"Good morning, Mr. Chandler." The butler accepted the guest's hat and his cane. "Sir Christopher is in the library, sir."

"Thank you." Martin smiled and took his time walking

through the house knowing there wouldn't be any unpleasant, accidental meetings with ex-fiancée Victoria. Since their broken engagement, Kit had conveniently relocated her to Bath.

"Didn't expect to see you so soon." Martin rounded the corner to find Kit at his desk penning a letter. "But I must admit I was glad to hear of it. Thank you for your message."

"Lady Frances was in a hurry to return home, can't say I blame her." Kit set his quill in the stand, leaving his correspondence unfinished, and Martin did not feel one bit guilty.

He stood next to the desk with his fist lightly resting on the surface. "Was it true, then? Is Russell Crawford guilty of making off with Lady Frances?"

"I'm afraid so." Kit leaned back in his chair.

"What did Sir Russell have to say for himself?"

"Never had a chance to ask, I'm afraid. He was beaten to a bloody pulp by the time I arrived."

"You don't say? Who was the miscreant?" With the positive outcome of the journey and the safe return of Lady Frances Abbott, Martin found it acceptable to make light of the horrid event.

"Mr. Albert Winslow."

"I'm afraid I'm not acquainted with him." Was this *Mr. Winslow* a hired thug Kit had brought along to subdue Sir Russell?

"You will be soon enough. He's a *cousin* of mine." Kit stood and indicated the lines of his family tree by movements in the air with his fingers.

"Another one?"

"He is the son of my mother's eighth husband Lord Beeson's sister who married a Mr. Alfred Winslow." It was astonishing how easily the branches and limbs of his family tree rolled from Kit's memory.

As if any of that nonsense made the connection understandable, Martin would merely take Kit at his word. To refer to Albert Winslow as *cousin* was acceptable enough.

"I brought Albee back with me from Bath. Couldn't leave him in the house with those three ladies." Kit's shrug indicated his amiable nature. "His aunt who had the devil of a time getting her way, my mother who could have persuaded him to do anything, and Vic who would have had him on the end of a lead in two days' time."

What was Kit to do?

Martin understood completely. It was probably best that Winslow came to Town with Kit.

"Shall we sit and catch up?" Kit stood from his desk and strolled to the tall windows overlooking the back garden and motioned for him to take the nearby chair. "There was so much going on and I had to make quick arrangements. I would like to thank your family for taking in Jane during my absence. Mrs. Chandler has been most accommodating."

"Mother was delighted to help. Jane and Pauline rub along so well, it was no imposition at all." The two girls were good company for one another, even after the dissolution of his engagement to Victoria. His was a small part played in the recent two families' drama. "And I fulfilled your obligation as escort with Lady Emmeline. Do you have any further plans regarding her?"

"Lady Emmeline!" Kit stilled, his eyes widened. He thumped his forehead with his index and middle fingers. "Gad, with everything that's been going on, she had completely slipped my mind."

"Yet you managed to set her squarely on my plate before you left." Martin would not soon forget.

"That was because I was standing on Arlington Street

waiting for her. I didn't feel it right to abandon her without explanation."

"So you sent me." Martin had felt that was the worst—no, the most *arduous* day of his life. It even exceeded the day of Kit's duel with Linwood. "Lady Emmeline was none too happy with me as your replacement."

"Was she really? She is so amiable, I thought she could get on with almost anyone."

"I did not find her agreeable." Martin thought of many other adjectives to describe her but kept them to himself.

"I am shocked to hear you say so, Martin."

The very idea of spending time with her made him uncomfortable. "What were you thinking? I wouldn't expect you to care for someone of *that* nature."

"I can't imagine what you mean. She's charming, beautiful... there is something...an intangible quality." Kit paused as if he needed to invent new ethereal words to describe her. "I, and I believe many other men, find her quite enchanting. I am amazed that you do not share our opinion."

"*Enchanting* is not the word I would use. No." Martin thought he had spent enough time and effort on the topic of Lady Emmeline and wanted to discuss her no more. "I only wanted to inform you that I successfully carried out your commitments to her. There are no subsequent arrangements for you two to meet. I thought I'd leave that to you."

"Thank you, Martin." Kit sounded sincere. "I apologize for the inconvenience. I had not meant it to task you. You were merely a Gentleman to help out his friend."

"I suppose there is nothing truly *wrong* with her," Martin said at last. "No. You may care for her but I believe she isa female not to my taste."

THE DAY AFTER HER RETURN, FRANCES' THREE CLOSEST FRIENDS called at Langford House to welcome her home.

"Lady Langford said you were ready to receive visitors." Cousin Jane spoke softly as she, Miss Chandler, and Lady Emmeline entered Frances' bedchamber.

"I am well." Frances assured them with a bit of a forced smile, but she was not the same, not inside.

When Frances returned home two nights ago, it was a low-keyed welcome. Her parents Lord and Lady Langford drew their beloved eldest daughter into their arms and hugged her tightly. Frances would have liked to have promised she would never, ever leave their side ever again except her departure from London was not her choice.

She had been *taken*. *Stolen* from her family.

Next to her family, what she truly valued was the company of her new friends. How kind they were to all come together and it would be as it was *before*.

Mrs. Chandler sent a box of small cakes in care of Miss Chandler for the group to enjoy while they had a nice visit. Lady Emmeline brought a small bouquet of violets that Frances had placed on her nightstand, next to her, in a small glass bottle. Miss Stiles loaned her one of her favorite books, hoping Frances might spend some quiet hours reading an uplifting story while she continued to recover.

Her friends were all so lovely. Their visit did cheer her.

While on the Great North Road Frances had not given them a single thought, these three ladies who now surrounded her. Being in their company again made her very happy. Yet, she could not dare share everything that had happened.

Frances was never to see her old life as it was again. She had no wish to dwell upon that dreadful day but she felt as though, try as she might, she could not move past the incident.

"It must have been horrible for you." Lady Emmeline was a bit older than the other two might have guessed what dangers Frances faced.

"We were so worried," Cousin Jane told Frances. "We did not wish to speculate but there was so much unknown to us. Kit told me only bits and pieces before he and Mr. Winslow left to find you."

"We waited ever so long, seemed like ages," Miss Chandler continued.

"By the next morning there was a letter from Kit saying they had found you and you would be on your way home." Cousin Jane sighed. "It seemed as if we waited forever for it to be over and then it was."

There was a lull in the conversation.

"I did not know Sir Russell but I cannot imagine what kind of monster would steal you away." Lady Emmeline sounded as if she were close to tears.

"I would not think him capable of such." Frances thought she had known him but, as it turned out, she did not know him at all.

"What has happened to him?" Miss Chandler's question was for anyone who could answer.

"Kit said there was a fight and he was knocked unconscious." Cousin Jane had the right of it but lacked the details.

"By Sir Christopher?" Lady Emmeline wondered aloud.

"Will Sir Russell be arrested for what he's done?" Miss Chandler seemed a bit worried.

"I cannot say." Frances did not wish to add to any speculation because she truly did not know.

"He should be. It's against the law to kidnap people," Lady Emmeline stated in no uncertain terms.

Kidnap sounded so serious but that is exactly what had happened to her. Frances had been kidnapped. "I'm sure my father will see to the legalities."

Cousin Jane leaned over and hugged Frances. "I'm so glad you're back."

Miss Chandler rose from her chair to join in on the hug. "Safe and unharmed."

Not to be left out, Lady Emmeline was the last to wrap her arms around the three and added, "How lucky we are to have one another for friends."

After their short visit, her three friends bid Frances farewell and left. She returned to her place of isolation and sadness. Perhaps staying inside, away from others, was not the best medicine for her. Saunders had kept her company so Frances would not be alone. Together they read, chatted, and took short walks in the rear gardens. Frances wasn't entirely certain it was enough.

The "something" that happened to Frances could not be conveyed, not to her three friends, not to her parents, not even to Saunders. It was a thing that had no words and she doubted that anyone could understand even if she had tried to explain. She wanted to keep the thoughts and feelings of it at bay...to prevent the fear of it returning, creeping into her brain.

The atmosphere around Frances felt tense. It was something she felt mostly when she was alone. It was as if the world around her had turned dark, ominous. She did not wish to think the world was a bad place.

Would she ever recover from her trauma? Frances could not prevent her thoughts from returning and prayed that those feelings would ebb. More than anything she wanted it all forgotten.

two

ADDED TO HIS ROUND of obligatory calls, Christopher needed to stop at Kennington House in hopes for an audience with Lady Emmeline. He had no idea how he could have forgotten about her upon his return to Town and had delayed his visit for longer than he ought.

Upon stepping inside, Christopher was struck with the sheer number of flowers that filled the entry hall. Never had he seen so many bouquets and arrangements except in a florist shop. He spotted some that were the exact color of his waistcoat and another that inspired an idea for a subsequent garment.

If these tributes were from Lady Emmeline's plethora of admirers then he felt no guilt in ignoring her for these last few days, perhaps his presence was not even missed.

"Sir Christopher, it has been an age." Lady Kennington approached to greet him.

"Good day to you, my lady." He touched the brim of his hand and performed a slow nod. "I was hoping to find Lady Emmeline At Home this morning."

"You have indeed. She is in her bedchamber finishing her

toilette. Would you care to wait in the front parlor?" Lady Kennington motioned to a pair of open double doors.

"Thank you." Christopher removed his hat but kept hold of it. He did not wish to overstay his welcome and hoped he would not occupy the lovely Lady Emmeline's time for more than ten minutes.

He followed Lady Kennington into the front parlor. He was taken aback by an additional number of floral tributes that filled the room. It was certain that Lady Emmeline did not lack admirers.

"I wish to apologize for my absence these last few days. I was called away on an emergency, family matters."

"I am sorry to hear that. I hope the resolution was to your satisfaction."

"All has been set to rights and I can resume the delights of my Season." Christopher pointedly gazed around the room. "I regret that I could not keep my social engagements to Lady Emmeline. My very good friend Martin Chandler was kind enough to fulfill my commitments."

"Yes, Emmeline has told me as much." Lady Kennington did not sound pleased. Whether this was a personal assessment or a reflection of how Lady Emmeline felt was yet to be seen. "Won't you be seated. She may be some time yet."

Christopher could just imagine. He had been warned about her *punctual* nature. He settled on the sofa and noticed that her ladyship did not sit.

"You must own, Sir Christopher, that Mr. Chandler may have taken your place, I do not believe he could have, in any way, replaced you."

With that Lady Kennington left him to wait.

EMMELINE HAD BEEN TOLD OF SIR CHRISTOPHER'S ARRIVAL. SHE had mixed feelings about seeing him again. There was nothing for it since he was here. By the time she had finished her toilette, Em found him waiting in the front parlor.

He stood when she entered the room, followed by her mother. "Lady Emmeline." With a slow nod of his head, he acknowledged her. He was very much a Gentleman. That, she thought, must always be admired.

"Sir Christopher," she replied, lowering into a curtsy. Em, still a bit vexed regarding his unexpected absence and perhaps slightly annoyed at his abrupt arrival, would have thought she might have been more pleased to see him but alas...she did not feel that way.

"I'm sure you two have much to say to one another." Lady Kennington made her presence known. "I'll leave you two now, shall I?"

"Thank you, Mama." Em seated herself on the opposite side of the same sofa that Sir Christopher had occupied. With one last look over her shoulder, she noted that her mother made certain the doors were left wide open before strolling down the corridor.

We must observe the proprieties, and it would not have been improbable that Mrs. Peckover lurked somewhere behind a door or a curtain.

Without any preconceived notions of what he might say or what her reaction might be, Em allowed Sir Christopher to initiate the conversation.

"You look well, my lady." The manner in which he regarded

her seemed most sincere. He did not seem overly eager to share her company despite his absence.

"Thank you, sir," she replied. Em allowed a small smile to touch the corners of her mouth.

"I came here to beg your forgiveness for abandoning you without notice." If he had missed her, perhaps she might find that she missed him as well, but he did not say so. It was all rather disappointing.

"You did not abandon me outright." She met his gaze now. "You sent Mr. Chandler in your stead."

"Yes, Martin did me the favor of escorting you for those delightful occasions we had hoped to spend time together."

"Yes..." was her weak reply. "And he was...." *Adequate* was the word that came to mind but it sounded so very lacking as a description. Em did not find Mr. Chandler in any way agreeable. The best she could say is that he was *pleasant*. "A most entertaining diversion."

"I am glad to hear that. I hope you found him amusing."

"Oh, yes, very amusing." *And maddening.* "We managed to get along well enough without you."

"How lowering to discover one is so easily replaced." Christopher glanced down at the carpet and she wondered if she'd wounded him.

"I am sorry," Em whispered. She kept her polite smile fixed and wondered what it was she had seen in this man. He was wildly popular with many but for Em.... She observed him closely.

Sir Christopher was not *that* handsome. Nor was he *that* charming.

Their time apart had certainly given her a clearer perspective. What exactly had she seen in him that she thought to monopolize his time?

Was it his sudden popularity had made him desirable to her? Everyone wanted to be with him and that was easy enough for Em. She knew how to turn men's heads and gain their attention.

Spending time with the baronet now, just in these few minutes, she quickly found him a bit...*boring*? Was that the correct word? *Dull*? It didn't matter, she decided she would no longer waste any of her time in his company.

Sir Christoper might have had a chance with her at one time.... No, she corrected herself. He had never had a chance with her, not really.

"Would you care to accompany me for a drive tomorrow?" he politely offered. She bore him no ill-will, it was simply she no longer had the slightest bit of interest in him.

"I am sorry." Em did not need to create an excuse for her time as she was genuinely occupied for the next fortnight.

Many would still find Sir Christopher pleasing and she felt certain that he would easily secure some other lady's interest. But not hers. Em now had her own circle of acquaintances and as agreeable as he was, she did not find him to her taste.

"Perhaps we will meet at the Everett's Ball?" he suggested.

"Perhaps we will." She had no wish to outright refuse him.

"And share a dance?" he offered.

"I look forward to it." If he were still as popular as he had been, if she were to be seen dancing with him.... It would certainly do both of their reputations much good. She stood to signal the end of his visit and offered him her hand. "I bid good day to you, Sir Christopher."

"And to you, Lady Emmeline." He rose and accepted her hand, bowed over it before taking his leave.

THAT EVENING, CHRISTOPHER AND ALBEE WERE VERY PLEASED TO accept a dinner invitation from Lord and Lady Langford. This was not a party but more of a *gathering* for the pair to renew their hasty acquaintance and to show the gentlemen proper appreciation for what they had done. They hadn't seen the family since returning Lady Frances a week ago.

The earl and countess stood to one side of the front parlor of their South Audley Street residence with Christopher while Albee sat quietly with Lady Frances near the hearth where they quietly conversed.

"I want to personally thank you, Sir Christopher and your friend Mr. Winslow, for everything you've done. You have gone above and beyond the call of Gentlemen. You have saved my daughter and my family." Lord Langford's voice became soft, hoarse with emotion.

"Your family *is* my family, your lordship. I will never forget that we are related." No matter how tenuous the connection, Christopher held all his relations close to his heart. If it were not for tenuous connections he would have very few family members indeed.

"*Relations*...I suppose we are." Lord Langford narrowed his eyes in contemplation. "As for Sir Russell...the law will see to his punishment. At the moment, I am more concerned with my daughter's well-being."

"As you should be," agreed Christopher.

"Look at those two," Lady Langford cooed, referring to her daughter and Albee. "They do appear to be enjoying their coze."

"Sharing a trauma sometimes brings people together." Christopher could think of no more deserving man than his friend. If he could find happiness with Lady Frances all the better for him.

"What can you tell me about Mr. Winslow?" Lord Langford

turned to a matter of more interest. Lady Frances had experienced difficulties with her prior two fiancés. One could understand his lordship's concern over a potential third.

"I have known Albert Winslow for a good fifteen years now, first as a boy then as a man. He has always been an honest, hardworking sort. He lives a quiet life and keeps to himself, caring for his estate in Somerset—"

"Ah, Somerset, that's not too far from Shropshire." Lord Langford sounded encouraged with the proximity to his own country house.

"—Which, I understand, earns approximately twenty thousand a year," Christopher informed him. A healthy income would prove a beneficial quality for any potential son-in-law.

"Twenty thousand! Why that is—" Lady Langford lowered her voice. "Quite excellent."

"Are you marrying Lady Frances off so soon?" Christopher would have thought a bit more prudence might be called for. She had just been through quite an ordeal.

"I think their match is inevitable." Lord Langford must have seen the writing on the wall. "He has already spoken to me about courting her."

"Has he?" Lady Langford appeared surprised at Albee's interest.

Christopher thought it was understandable considering his friend's past. "I should caution you that Mr. Winslow is not one to allow an opportunity pass. He has a very much *life is short, it is not to be wasted* outlook." Christopher could just imagine once Albee had fallen in love he would waste no time and wed the lady in a thrice.

Mr. Winslow sat rather close to Frances near the hearth. She did not mind, it actually surprised her that she found his presence of such comfort.

"You are looking well, Lady Frances," he said encouragingly. "Quite well, actually." A smile came easy to him. His kind eyes appeared much brighter than she remembered.

"And you look much more the thing, Mr. Winslow," Frances returned, she felt her cheeks warm.

"Thank you. I am improving." He glanced down at his gloved hands and flexed them. "They are still not ready to be seen. I'm afraid I've injured them quite badly."

The recent memory of how he had used his fists had not faded. The fine, light brown-colored leather gloves were a bit unusual for indoor wear but understandable. The fingers appeared to fit snugly, indicating the swelling beneath.

"I had thought to call sooner but.... I thought you needed time to recuperate and did not wish to disturb you and your family during this period." His soft voice was gentle and his manner toward her most amiable. "I was glad to see the dinner invitation from your parents."

"They are quite grateful to you and Sir Christopher, as am I." Frances tried to keep from thinking that his concern for her well-being might be more than general concern. Perhaps he thought because he saved her that he was somehow responsible for her welfare. *Well, that was nonsense.*

"There is no use for any overwhelming gratitude."

"But my family and I *are* grateful. However, I fear I may be entrenched in scandal again." Frances did not wish to dwell upon it. "It seems no matter what I do, it follows."

"You have done nothing to bring this upon yourself. It is a chain of misfortunes you have suffered." He glanced at her, drew in a deep breath, and straightened his posture directing his answer to her in a direct and most honest manner. "I cannot say your reputation matters to me. For I know the truth of the matter."

"If you do not let it concern you, sir." Frances gently placed her hand atop his gloved one and smiled. How could she prevent herself from finding a soft part in her heart for him? "Then it shan't matter to me either."

three

FOR A SMALL RESPITE from the rounds of parties and engagements, Emmeline had decreed that she was not At Home this morning, thus giving her some time to consider the potential suitors who wished to share her company.

Mrs. Peckover entered the room with a small basket filled with the morning's invitations. "Are you ready, Lady Emmeline? I have called for tea and Lady Kennington will join us momentarily." She settled herself on the far end of the sofa and set the basket upon her lap.

Again? Em sighed at the task ahead of her. All she wanted was to bask in the adoration of her admirers...just for a bit.

"There are so many. How is one to choose?" Em glanced over Mrs. Peckover's shoulder as she flipped through.

"One allows one's mother to first sort through them, of course," Mrs. Peckover replied.

It would be only minutes until Lady Kennington arrived and the three would go through the small stack of envelopes. It was such a chore.

Em wished to enjoy her Season, knowing it would be her

only one. She would, no doubt, marry soon. All she need do is choose amongst the gentlemen around her. And there were so many handsome gentlemen who sent beautiful flowers in hopes of gaining her attention. She scanned the floral tributes that lined the surfaces of the front parlor and strolled among them while waiting for her mother.

A few specific bouquets had caught her eye. She found the hot house varieties interesting. The mignonette and grenadine, very nice. The dianthus mixed pale pink peonies, she thought lovely. And, always a favorite of hers because of the scent, were the lilacs. But the flowers were not indicative of the sender.

She stepped closer to read some of the accompanying cards: Mr. Lester, Sir Thomas Selby, Lord Gower, Lord Edward Shaw. Any of these gentlemen might do, perhaps all of them were contenders.

Em smiled.

To be honest. She was not quite certain. A select few had been singled out and referred to as her *beau* this last fortnight but she could not say she was pleased with any of them. Nothing was more enjoyable than attending parties where her acquaintances, of both sexes, congregated and paid her much attention. She secretly confessed to herself that finding one particular gentleman which she would love, respect, and cherish had eluded her.

Perhaps she was asking for too much. Perhaps she thought it might be easier than it would be. Perhaps she needed to be more patient.

That young man might not arrive for another week yet, maybe two. If so, Em should steady herself for duration and not prove to be a flighty female who accepted the first seemingly acceptable gentleman that came along.

Emmeline was willing to wait for just the right man. Hopefully, he would stand out from the rest and be instantly known to her.

She continued around the room, admiring the flowers and taking in their heavenly scents. It was as if she were walking through an indoor garden. The more colorful or more impressive displays did not always mean an importance in station, nor did it indicate someone harboring a deeper affection.

One arrival had caught Em's attention and she intended to keep watch for it, finding it unusual. She moved around the room until...*there it was.*

Secluded in the far end of the room, not in a particularly prominent position, between two other, much taller, arrangements that dwarfed a small, simply glazed, earthenware pot. Em found this plant exquisite. The broad dark-green shiny leaves provided the perfect background for the white camellia. Originating from the East, she understood this type of exotic plant grew in a glass house.

Sometimes the smaller, more simple offerings were preferred. It was certainly true in this case. Her personal preference was for something that was not particularly so grand but unique. Of course none of the men would have been privy to that.

This beautiful white camellia with its perfectly round petals was her favorite. Then she noticed one of the heavy, weighty blossoms had proved too much for its stem and had fallen, lying face down on the table.

Em lifted the flower, turned it to find the blossom intact, still perfect. Retaining its beauty, it would be a shame to throw it away. She would find a crystal dish and place it in a small amount of water and set it upon the low table in the parlor where she could admire it while seated on the sofa. It would be off by itself and she could look upon it without the distraction of the others.

"What have you there, my lady?" Mrs. Peckover spied Em's prolonged interest in the blossom she'd rescued.

"Just a camellia flower that's fallen from its stem. You wouldn't happen to know who sent them, would you? I did not find a card."

"Let me see...." The chaperone set the basket on her lap aside and left for only a moment before returning with a few sheets of paper. "I've made notes of who has sent which and...." She scanned the list. "Let me see...eh...that is from...Mr. Chandler."

Martin Chandler? How could she prefer *his* flowers to anyone else's? This was an outrage. Emmeline stomped her foot, completely vexed with herself.

"IF PAULINE AND JANE ARE TO KEEP ONE ANOTHER COMPANY AND they are accompanied by you and Mrs. H," Martin justified. He had no wish to remain at Lady Chesney's residence, a place that held such unpleasant memories. Memories that were created only a week ago. "I see no need for me to stay."

"You have a point." Kit agreed. "There is no point in having the chaperones outnumber the charges."

"I have no wish to tag along as if I were some sort of lap dog," he grumbled. "I can't for the life of me understand why I am here."

"I think your mother would like to see you out of the house for a change," Mrs. Heffelfinger retorted rather sharply. Perhaps older ladies feel the need to *mother* even if the *child* was not her own.

Kit looked from Mrs. Heffelfinger to Martin, somewhat taken aback by their interaction. Not that he was of an age of a child, but Martin certainly behaved in a petulant manner much resembling one.

"I rather fancy a *brisk* walk than the meanderings of two silly young ladies who stop and smell every flower and an *old* woman."

Mrs. Heffelfinger took great offense at the word *old*, clutching her throat and gasping.

"There is no reason to be rude, Martin. Go on. Off with you." Kit motioned for him to proceed down the path. "Take your *brisk* walk. Can I rely on you *not* to walk off in a sulk?"

Martin rolled his eyes, grumbled, and advanced, moving away. In his pique, he heard them clearly from a distance.

"I wouldn't have thought his broken engagement still bothered him. One would think it had only happened yesterday."

What set Martin off had not happened yesterday but the week before. So, if it had occurred a week ago, why was he still in the midst of the blue devils?

JANE AND PAULINE WALKED ARM IN ARM, CHRISTOPHER FOLLOWED, walking alongside Mrs. Heffelfinger on one of the paths in Lady Chesney's expansive rear garden of her London residence. Last week there had been a Venetian Breakfast, this week another activity, although he was not exactly certain *what,* had been planned.

There was no telling who would attend which caused him to believe this event was akin to a ramshackle event. Perhaps there was something to be said for a strict, orderly guest list. It kept the riffraff away. Watching over the two young ladies, who have yet to be Out, it seemed to him that even more care needed to be exercised than if they had attended their first Season.

Jane and Pauline, these two young ladies strolling before him had one foot in the schoolroom, inexperienced and somewhat naive, and one foot in Town in the pretense of fashionable Misses.

"Have you seen Lady Frances recently?" Pauline's last visit had been when they had all gone together a few days before.

"Not since the day the three of us called on her together." Jane amended, "Kit and Albee have dined with Lady Frances and her parents just last night."

"He is still *Mr. Winslow*, to you." Christopher corrected, not wishing his sister to become too familiar with his friend.

"It's *Albee*," Jane whispered to Pauline who giggled.

Silly females.

"Did you find Lady Frances well, Sir Christopher?" Pauline still faced forward when she spoke, waiting for his reply.

"She seemed very well. Quite recovered." Christopher would never admit that Albee had taken a good share of Cousin Frances' time, and he would not argue that she did not mind in the least.

"That is very good to hear," Pauline replied. "What of Mr. Winslow?"

"What-*cha* mean?" Christopher thought hers was an odd question. Albee had not sustained any injury. None that these two would have knowledge at any rate.

"Since your return Mr. Winslow has seemed to keep to himself. I thought, perhaps, he was much preoccupied. I would like to think he's taken a fancy to Lady Frances."

Jane gasped. "Do you really think so?"

"He saved her life, didn't he?" Pauline swung her gaze from

Christopher to Jane. "If it's possible that she's enamored with him...could it be he is equally as enamored with her?"

"You're right." Jane appeared to have come to a realization. "I had not thought of that."

"On the topic of *earls' daughters*.... Do you know who Lady Emmeline fancies?" It would seem that Miss Know-It-All Pauline had an idea and intended to tease his sister.

"I do," Jane said confidently. "Lord Andrew Pelham."

"No. Sir Charles Hudson."

Jane shook her head. "She told me she thought she was 'rather fond' of Lord Andrew Pelham."

"That cannot be." Pauline sounded as if she were growing rather cross. "Lady Emmeline told me she was 'half in love' with Sir Charles Hudson."

"Lord Andrew Pelham."

"Sir Charles Hudson."

"Ladies, does it truly matter?" Christopher did not wish to hear the bickering of two girls. "I'm sure she has had time to have a change of heart. As far as you know Lady Emmeline could be favoring a third or fourth gentleman by now."

"Sir Christopher has the right of it." Mrs. Heffelfinger who trailed the group, walking alongside Christopher, spoke louder as to be heard. "When you're young you can be as fickle as the direction of the wind. In one's youth, ladies are known to change affection as often as their frock. Do not take offense, you both may be correct."

The chaperone's words seemed to have fallen by the wayside for the two returned to their quibbling.

"Lord Andrew Pelham," Jane insisted, whispering.

"Sir Charles Hudson," again corrected Pauline.

"Do forget about Lady Emmeline's preference. Why do we not return home and write to Lady Frances. I'm certain she would greatly favor some news. Perhaps you can learn more about her budding romance with" —Mrs. Heffelfinger glanced at Christopher before she whispered— *"Albee."*

"Mrs. Heffelfinger!" Christopher chided the older woman. "Where are your manners!"

It made all the females around him giggle.

Rapid footfalls approached from behind. The group turned back toward the house to see a footman approaching. He looked rather in a hurry, and he was out of breath.

Christopher merely waited for the footman's arrival. As he waited he noticed multiple black and red liveried footmen running from the back of the house into every corner of the garden, finding each guest.

"What is it?"

"Sir, I am to inform you that the Dancing Master has arrived! Instruction will begin just outside of the hour."

"Dancing Master?" Both Jane and Pauline brightened.

"What does that mean?" Jane asked the lad for clarification.

"Lady Chesney has arranged for Monsieur Philippe, lately of Paris, to provide instruction this afternoon in the ballroom for the guests who wish to participate." The footman had caught his breath and stated, "I beg your pardon. I must continue."

Christopher waved him forward and the footman raced off looking for other guests.

"A Dancing Master!" Pauline's excitement could not be contained. "I've never had a proper lesson. I should love to attend."

"We've had one who visited. It was years ago," Jane told her friend. "He came to the house once a week for a few months, I believe, before Victoria's Season. *We* will need to learn before our Come Out. May we attend, Kit?"

"Oh, yes. I would like that above all things." Pauline's eyes were filled with hope, she was eager to attend and had no wish to miss out on the fun.

Christopher could not imagine Martin refusing Pauline. He could not very well say Yes to Jane and No to her. When he returned her gaze, it struck him how little determination he had to refuse her.

Both she and Pauline turned to Christopher. "Shall we return to the house?"

These two were determined to plant both feet in the present of London as young adults. It appeared that Christopher would not be able to stop them.

four

WHAT ON EARTH MADE him attend the Everett ball? Martin had no need to attend any type of party. It was Kit who'd asked for his company and wished to introduce his longtime friend Albert Winslow.

But why at a ball? Why not simple introductions at Grayson House?

After he had made Mr. Winslow's acquaintance, Martin parted ways with them. He would have liked to have left but promised Kit he would remain, if for no other reason than to keep Albert Winslow company.

Martin felt restless and excused himself to find some fresh air, promising to return. He stepped away but was still subjected to *all these other people.* As unfortunate as that was there was one particular person he'd rather not see—Lady Emmeline Cordia-Darling. It was difficult to say if he wished to avoid her more than she wished to avoid him.

The fact of the matter was they simply did not get on.

To escape the crush in one of the reception rooms, he had thought he'd cut through the ballroom and slip out the back to find the Gentlemen's withdrawing room. There before him, on the dance floor, in a white gown covered with a shimmering overskirt was Emmeline. It was as if she was illuminated with a light from within, unfairly distinguishing her from the other females around her.

The worst part of it was...he could not take his eyes from her. He did not wish to notice her for Martin knew her to be not what she appeared...enchanting and beautiful, tinged with something not so savory.

Sir Garrett Hudson partnered her in a country dance. She smiled at him and whispered something when they came together. He smiled when they parted, leaving Sir Garrett to stand taller, more confident...perhaps *over*-confident. She did something to him to make him behave as if he were invincible.

What had she said to him? That he was the most handsome man in attendance? That she cared for him above all others?

Martin was not jealous...it was only that he did not think any good could come of their interaction. The episode was unusually unsettling and he did not understand why.

The set came to an end and the floor began to clear. Martin discarded the notion of finding fresh air and opted to seek out his two friends.

"Had you hoped for a dance with Lady Emmeline?" Martin murmured to Kit when he'd found him. "You'd better have a move on, she might not even have a dance left for you."

"Well, I had thought—" Kit swiftly excused himself to see if he could claim a dance with her.

"I don't think I've ever seen him so shaken." Albert Winslow chuckled and took great care smoothing his gloves over his fingers and the palms of his hands.

"Now I know his reasons for attending, what are yours?"

Chandler asked. "You're not interested in standing in the petticoat line, as far as I know."

"You have the right of it there." Why *had* Albert attended the Ball? "I wanted to keep my friend company, I supposed." He glanced at Chandler. "Two friends, if I may be so bold."

Martin Chandler smiled. "What is it they say? A friend of my friend is *my* friend?"

Albert bowed his head. That was a high compliment indeed.

"Perhaps a more apt reason for Kit's presence is to regain Lady Emmeline's good graces. He says they did not part on the best terms." Albert gazed across the room but could not see where Kit had gone. "What do you think his chances are?"

"It depends if she believes him to be *useful* to her."

"*Useful?*" Albert was somewhat taken aback by the bluntness of Chandler's words. "That sounds absolutely mercenary."

"You asked me, my friend. I am giving you my honest opinion." No smile that hinted of sarcasm accompanied his reply. "My opinion of her is not favorable. There is something about her that rings of *duplicity.*"

"That sounds rather harsh." It was Albert's understanding that Kit was not looking for a wife but Lady Emmeline could have been the very one who changed his mind. But if what Chandler said was true....

The two men stood together and watched their friend return some minutes later. Kit looked to be a bit deflated.

He stepped between his two friends and announced, "She won't have me."

"There you see," Chandler whispered to Albert. "No, surprise there, Kit. You've treated her badly."

"She's been ill-treated, you say?" This must have been a revelation to Kit.

"You abandoned her."

"I did no such thing." Kit appeared to take great offense at the accusation. "I provided an adequate escort in my absence. I called upon my return, fairly soon after, and apologized."

"You left her in the care of another." Chandler's reaction seemed to indicate it was an insufficient action. "And one who did not care a fig about her well-being."

"But it was you.... I left you to—"

"Ah...you think me *adequate*.... I do not believe *she* believes me close to that."

"Are you telling me...telling me *now* that I must suffer *your* ill-handling of her?"

"Quite possibly," Chandler admitted. "It still does not excuse your neglect and it would not surprise me if that is all she notices."

"Are you telling me your actions were my fault?" Kit appeared absolutely nonplussed.

"I did what I could." Chandler shrugged. "It would seem that she is not the girl for you."

"From what you've said, Chandler, she may not be the girl for anyone," Albert added.

"That, Mr. Winslow, may be more true that you know." Chandler turned his attention to Kit. "You'd be best to get over her, I'm afraid she's moved on...does not lack for suitors, you know."

"No, I suppose not." Kit repeated, eyeing the court that surrounded her even from where they stood across the room. "Do not give up on love, Martin. I certainly will not—when I am ready to take that step."

"Give up?" Chandler balked at the remark. "I am not so certain if such a thing exists."

"You cannot blame Victoria for leading you astray. That may have been something else entirely."

"More akin to what Lady Emmeline has done to you?"

"Perhaps...." If men could blush...that is what Kit did. "But not to the same extent. Our friend Albee has been inflicted to suffer a fate that left him devastated, but I am convinced that Cupid's arrow may have pierced his heart again."

"Really?" Chandler turned and gazed at his new acquaintance with fresh eyes. "And *who* might she be?"

Kit made no attempt to restrain himself and her name came freely from his lips, "Lady Frances Abbott."

"Ah...the young lady you recently rescued." The rate in which Chandler could relate the two was startling.

"What news do you have regarding Lady Frances, Albee?" Kit had successfully deflected the direction of their conversation away from him. "Did you call on her this morning?"

"I did." Winslow could not keep from smiling. "We strolled together in the rear gardens. I hope the excursions will help her grow stronger so she and I will eventually be able to dance. I know there is quite a way to go yet."

"I believe you will make a great difference in her recovery," Kit replied, actually it was a compliment. "I expect she will improve in no time."

"She is becoming quite dear to me. I did not think I could ever feel this way about someone...not so soon after.... It's been wholly unexpected."

"Do not despair, my friend." Kit clapped his friend on the shoulder. "*Affection* does not ask permission...it merely *is*."

"Gad! *Affliction*...I would say." Chandler shook his head. Had he given up on finding love? He had no notion to even look.

Life didn't need to be that way, it changed. It had for Albert. He wished there were some words of comfort he could share. Circumstances would improve when one least expected it.

31

"Take no mind of Martin, Albee" Kit whispered. "He suffered at Victoria's hands not so long ago."

"I don't think I can tolerate either of you...thoroughly *smelling of April and May*." Chandler glanced around, looking for an escape, no doubt. It wasn't too much later that he politely excused himself and left.

MARTIN WALKED AWAY FROM KIT AND WINSLOW. HE DELIBERATELY avoided the ballroom and thought the best place for him would be in the Gentlemen's room. *She* would certainly not be in there.

"Not another one." Lord Gower eased into one of the leather chairs.

"All this talk of dueling is ridiculous." Lord Finch leaned back in his chair, puffing on his cigar after toasting the tip in a candle flame, and headed for the seat next to Gower. "Who were the two nitwits meeting on the field of honor?"

"Sir Milton Leech and Lord Peter Grant."

"And *what* were they dueling over?"

"The preferred preparation of beef...boiled or roasted." Gower grumbled, clearly not amused. "Another *farcical* duel."

"It's getting *demmed* tiresome." Finch puffed out a cloud of smoke. "When will it end?"

"Someday there'll be some nincompoop who'll have his head blown off and then they'll take the whole thing seriously."

Martin could not stand to hear another word and decided it was time for him to leave, with or without Kit and Winslow. Just as he reached the other side of the room an argument between two men erupted. He paused to observe. The shouting and shoving reached a point where it drew everyone's attention.

"You will not have her!" Lord Robert Blair proclaimed, his voice carried easily when the room fell quiet around them.

"That will be over my dead body. I will kill you with my bare hands." Sir Garrett grabbed Lord Robert's lapels and shook him quite violently. It looked to Martin that Sir Garrett was willing to dispense with the duel and go for outright fisticuffs.

"Gentlemen, *gentlemen*...." Someone who had a calmer head intervened. "This does no good to fight in the middle of a ball, and certainly not at Everett's. He, nor Mrs. Everett will thank you for making their home a battlefield."

"We can step over to Hyde Park, we'll find a decent spot. Won't be anyone there this time of night."

"We can't do that," someone else said. "What about the seconds, finding a compromise, and such?"

"There will be no satisfaction unless I am the only one left standing." The two next to Sir Garrett restrained him.

"Right here, right now, then," Lord Robert returned with equal venom. "If you refuse then you are a coward. Lady Emmeline will never have you."

Lady Emmeline? Had Martin heard that right? What did she have to do with this quarrel?

The anger and contempt was palpable, creating a compelling and highly charged scene. Martin found it nearly unfathomable that Emmeline's name should be uttered as grounds of this disagreement. If there was to be a duel in the morning, he felt compelled to attend. He wished to see the outcome.

This would be the second duel of the Season he'd observed, and sincerely hoped this would not become a habit. As Lord Finch said, 'all these duels were ridiculous.'

Lord Robert rushed past him, exiting—and Martin thought *he* was in a hurry to leave.

Martin followed in Lord Robert's path, somewhat reluctantly. He saw no need to dash off like some youngblood craving
vengeance, and it would not be on Lady Emmeline's behalf.
Martin would like to think he had more sense than that.

Coming to the end of the corridor that opened into a foyer at
the side of the house Martin saw Emmeline rushing up from
behind Lord Robert Blair, calling to him.

"My lord.... My lord...." From where had she come? Martin
also stopped, stepped back, and made no other move to retreat,
effectively eavesdropping on their privacy.

Was this another piece of the drama?

"*Emmeline....* Lady Emmeline." He took her hand and bowed.
Her presence caused Lord Robert's previous vitriol to fade and
he focused on her alone.

Emmeline had enchanted him and the man was completely
besotted with her. It was as if he were mesmerized. "I have heard
the most horrid thing." She sounded upset, very emotional,
Martin could hear the tremor in her voice.

"What is it, my lady?"

"Is it true? Are you to duel? *For me*?"

"You should not concern yourself. This is a matter between
two men."

"How you must care for me to...." Lady Emmeline lacked the
remorse in her voice Martin would have expected to hear.

"I do," Lord Robert assured her. "I care a great deal. *When* I
leave that field as the victor, there will be no doubt as to my
intentions."

She smiled and cast her gaze downward in a shy, mindful
manner. Martin could see her heightened blush from where he
stood and his suspicion was that she was not as innocent as to
what was to happen.

five

CHALK FARMS

"Seven! Eight! Nine! Ten!"

Both men turned to face one another. Lord Robert Blair stood calmly across from his opponent Sir Garrett Hudson. Martin had learned the two were equally matched which made the outcome less uncertain. They straightened their arms leveling their pistols toward the other taking aim. The morning was cool and dry. The visibility, good.

Martin waited next to the coach with the surgeon, well off the dueling field with the many other spectators. This would not be a farcical duel as was discussed last night. Neither of these gentlemen would delope. Their mood was serious, their expressions quite somber.

"For the hand of Lady Emmeline!" someone shouted.

Martin could feel the tension tighten as the seconds passed. They stood tall, their backs rigid, and they fought for the affections of Lady Emmeline. The winner might earn himself the right to ask for her hand in marriage. And what of the loser? His pride would certainly be bruised and he would be fortunate if that was the only wound sustained. If extremely lucky, he would walk away with his life.

Thinking back to last night, observing Lady Emmeline and Lord Robert, it occurred to Martin that she might have encouraged him. Certainly, she could not have anticipated *this*...nor wished him to duel. And had she somehow persuaded Sir Garrett to do the same?

Certainly not.

How could Emmeline have allowed this? How could Martin even contemplate that she actually influenced them into this? He couldn't imagine.

Yet here he was a spectator to see the outcome.

The anger of the two men remained, clearly etched onto the duelers' faces. If for some reason their weapons misfired or their shot went astray Martin could see them throwing aside their pistols and running into combat with their hands if need be.

Idiots! Young jackanapes! Neither man looked as if he were about to take aim away from their target. This was no joke as the other duels he'd heard of occurred days and weeks earlier. This was nothing short of deadly intent.

"Those gentlemen certainly seem as if they mean business." Mr. Braithwaite, the surgeon, whispered.

"Yes, sir. I believe they do." And that's what Martin feared most.

Both men held their pistols steady. It seemed neither showed weakness.

The simultaneous, ear-deafing BOOMS tore through the air followed by the smoke from the pistols. Sir Garrett Hudson dropped to his knees, clutching his arm while Lord Robert stood his ground and merely observed, savoring his triumph.

It took a few minutes before the smoke drifted slowly off the center of the field and dissipated. Mr. Braithwaite dashed onto the field to tend to Sir Garrett.

Cheers rang out for Lord Robert, his friends in the crowd congratulating him.

With a confirmed victor, and loser, the duel had come to an end. Martin expected that all might not turn out as well as expected.

Would this duel result in a scandal, unlike that of Sir Christopher's? Would there be an engagement announcement to follow? Would Lord and Lady Kennington absolutely forbid their daughter to become involved with such a miscreant that would subject their daughter to such an unfavorable actions? And what of the families? Was there no regard for them?

Indeed, the consequences from this duel had yet to be determined.

"LORD LANGFORD HAS BEEN MOST ACCOMMODATING, ALLOWING ME to hang about as I do." Mr. Winslow strolled at a nominal pace next to Frances in the rear gardens of Langford House.

He dressed not in the first stare of fashion but as a sensible gentleman. His preference was for buckskin breeches rather than fabric. He wore a well-fitting blue frock coat over a striped waistcoat, and his cravat was tied in a barrel knot. Of course he wore a pair of leather gloves, not as an accessory to his breeches but to cover his hands.

Mr. Winslow had offered his arm and Frances thought him most considerate. They proceeded to the rear gardens. He seemed to pay close attention to her, slowing when he felt as if she became fatigued.

"I must thank you for reading to me the other evening."

Frances welcomed his company and it pleased her that he accepted her request. "I've been reading such a great deal, it is a pleasure to hear someone else's voice for a change."

"The story became quite intriguing. I'm sorry we had to stop."

"End of the chapter you know...the next awaits." Frances smiled. "Miss Stiles was so kind as to lend me this book. She told me it was one of her favorites."

"As tempted as I am, I cannot see neglecting this glorious day by remaining indoors."

He was quite right. The afternoon was excellent...not too sunny, not too hot.... She enjoyed walking with Mr. Winslow immensely. She did not mind the limited area or the repetitive landscape...who noticed the shrubbery when there was such a handsome gentleman at one's side? To be honest, Frances did not always feel as if she physically struggled. It was only that she wished to prolong the outing to hold on to his arm or lean against him for support longer than she needed.

"You are not my only visitor, you know." She only thought to tease him a bit, although he did not seem to be the jealous type.

"Am I not?" And he did not seem surprised in the least and she could not outwit him to betray himself...to reveal what he felt for her.

Frances wondered if he found her as agreeable as she thought him. She had never met such a man: strong, protective, handsome. Perhaps she only thought him handsome because he had come to her rescue. It was her hope that that was not the only reason she felt as she has for him. Gratitude was no substitute for true affection.

"You must know that my cousin Jane, Miss Stiles, calls. She sometimes visits with her friend Miss Chandler, and at times they are accompanied by Lady Emmeline." Though, to be fair,

Lady Emmeline had quite a busy social schedule of her own. She must be very popular, Frances could not fault her for that.

"I thought you meant by other gentlemen." Did he mean to tease her back? "I thought there might be cause to be jealous."

"No, I don't believe there is." Frances could not admit that, even in a jest. "Since my return to London, my reputation has been on the edge of appearing questionable, hedging scandal it seems...even in those first days."

"Not by your doing."

"I may not have brought any of this on myself but the fact remains that I am not a paragon in Society, nowhere near that. All I wish is some respectability." Frances did not think it an unrealistic expectation.

Albert paused when they reached the small bench located next to the lawn that stretched behind the townhouse. "Shall we sit for a moment or two?" They remained well in-view to those that wished to ensure propriety was maintained. The *respectability* for which Lady Frances had spoke of, had hoped for.

They settled on the bench under a large-canopied tree, proving enough shade around them. Albert crossed his legs and rested the wrist of one hand on his knee while stretching his other arm along the back of the bench. Lady Frances took great care to arrange the folds of her skirts. A slight breeze made the occasion even more pleasant.

"This is lovely." She turned her head and closed her eyes, facing the moving air. A wisp of hair moved, fluttering gently against her cheek.

He gazed at her and returned, "This is *your* family's house." The surroundings must not have been unknown to her.

"But we do not command the weather, sir." Lady Frances smiled. "Perhaps you have brought that with you."

"I hardly think I can take credit for the weather, my lady." He chuckled.

Lady Frances glanced at his gloved hand, her expression became solemn. "How much longer will you need to wear them?"

"Until the bruising is gone. It's faded but it'll take a while longer before I will allow them to be seen in public. By the, people will merely think I've been spending my afternoons at Gentleman Jim's," he joked but when she did not seem to understand, he explained, "It's a Boxing Saloon."

"Oh," was her reply. "Do you think I might see?" He met her gaze, a nervous glance from her, uncertain but she was intrigued by what lay beneath.

Albert felt self-conscious. He didn't think it quite proper but he did not wish to openly refuse her. "Very well," he whispered and took great care removing the left glove, tugging gently on first the thumb, then each finger until he could easily slip it off with his palm facing toward them.

He watched her expression. Her gaze was fixed on his hand and when he rotated his wrist she observed the spots of dark purple bruising covering his knuckles. The color faded to red toward his fingers to nothing before reaching his wrist.

A small gasp escaped her at the sight. "Does it hurt?" As if she could not stop herself from doing so, Lady Frances gently brushed her fingertips against his tender, bruised skin.

"It's still a bit sore." He chuckled at her curiosity and felt a bit nervous, as he revealed his vulnerability. It was a reminder of his shameful behavior.

"I am sorry, Mr. Winslow." She pulled her hand away but could not keep from staring.

"*Albert*," he whispered. "It's my Christian name."

"*Albert*," she repeated, trying his name, and smiled as if she liked it.

"Or—you can call me Albee as Sir Christopher does." He wished she would call him anything but the overly formal Mister Winslow. He so wished to be on more casual terms with her.

"That is a boyhood name." Frances smiled and touched the glove covering his hand. "I much prefer *Albert*."

LADY EMMELINE CORDIA-DARLING ENTERED THE FRONT PARLOR OF Langford House where Lady Frances was good enough to receive her.

"Do be seated, Lady Emmeline." Lady Frances, because of her recuperation, had not greeted Em herself.

Em completely understood. She knew that entertaining the most welcome guest took much strength and was exhausting, she was not the first to arrive.

"Good morning, Lady Frances, I am very glad to see you up and about. Was that Mr. Winslow I saw leaving?" Em could think of no better tonic than Albert Winslow.

"Yes, it was." Lady Frances smiled. "Dear Lady Emmeline, you were so kind as to visit only a few days ago, and here you've returned. I'm sure you have so many other calls to pay."

"There are others, to be sure, but no one is more important. You have not stepped outside your own house for days. I cannot think of another who would benefit more from a friendly *Hello!*"

"You are really too kind." Lady Frances blushed. "Do tell me how you are finding your Season? Are you enjoying yourself? Is there a...have you met.... I do beg your pardon." She pressed her fingers to her mouth stifling the flow of words. "I am asking too many questions."

Although the two were not well acquainted, it was Em's wish that they could be better friends. She had hoped to learn something more of Frances' adventure north. There must have been some interesting story regarding the rescuer and the rescued. After all, the journey itself was days long. Long enough for some personal feelings to have developed.

"That is nonsense." Em poo-pooed Lady Frances' feelings that she should not speak her mind. "I do not know if we should speak openly whilst in the company of Miss Chandler or Miss Stiles but...I expect when it is just the two of us, I do not see any reason why we should not do so when we are private." Em offered Lady Frances an impish, mischievous smile. "There are no mothers, no chaperones. I believe there are certain topics that we young ladies wish to discuss and speak about without censure."

Certainly, there were things Emmeline wished to know.

She contemplated if any affection could develop between Lady Frances and Sir Christopher the leader of the rescue? No. Familiarity with each of them, and their natures, Em did not think that possible.

Perhaps there could be a connection between Lady Frances and Mr. Winslow? Something could already be stirring between those two. In the manner Lady Frances avoided Em's eye contact, accompanied by the deep blush at the mention of his name...she certainly held him in some regard.

"You are correct, Lady Emmeline. If I may be so bold...*Emmeline*," Lady Frances...*Frances* began. "There is great value speaking to someone my own age, someone who is not my mother.... Sometimes I think she cannot understand." Frances paused before saying, in a softer tone. "It may be that it has been quite some time since she has been—our age."

"Perhaps." Em thought that was a declaration that might have gone too far, and *she* would never repeat it to anyone. Yes, the two of *them* would keep these types of discussions to themselves.

"Mr. Winslow has been all that is kind. He wishes for my swift recovery and has accompanied me for a strolls in the rear gardens." She glanced down at her hands resting in her lap.

"How kind of him to take such an interest in you. How often have you walked together?"

"It has only been a few times but he has promised to see me follow a more strenuous routine." There was a softness in her eyes when she spoke of him. Had Frances realized she wasn't fooling anyone? It was obvious she'd already lost her heart. Em hoped Mr. Winslow felt the same for Frances, they seemed perfectly matched.

"His only wish is to share a dance or two with me before the end of the Season." It was as if Frances confessed a great secret.

"I don't expect that is his *only* wish." Em imagined it was the beginning of the two's budding romance. It was all very sweet.

Em knew very little of the newly arrived Mr. Winslow, besides being a very good friend of Sir Christopher. He was probably a nice sort but far too staid and probably lived in some country estate where he spent all his time. That was not the life for Emmeline.

"I do look forward to the time when we can attend the same balls and share dances with our Gentlemen," she amended, "Gentlemen-friends." Em did not currently have a beau but was certain she would soon favor another. She was hopeful.

"I look forward to it." In her excitement, Frances reached for

Em's hand and gave it a squeeze. "I hope it will not be much longer until I can attend. I do wish to keep my promises to both you and Mr. Winslow."

Six

"I DO NOT BELIEVE I am acquainted with him." Lord Kennington looked up from his desk in the library and shook his head, glancing at the calling card. "Never heard of him."

"Lord Robert is here to speak to you regarding Lady Emmeline, sir," the butler intone.

"*Emmeline?* Very well, Manfred, see him in." Kennington pushed his papers aside, intending to give Lord Robert his undivided attention. Well...this had to do with Emmeline and it could be an offer of marriage! She'd had them before but not from a London Gentleman. Perhaps this time it would be different.

"Lord Kennington." A young, well-dressed buck entered his lordship's library and bowed. "Lord Robert Blair, my lord. Perhaps you are familiar with my father the Duke of Ashcroft?"

"Ah, yes." Kennington had not met His Grace but the family was known to him.

"This morning I have won the right to address Lady Emmeline for her hand."

"*Won?* How's that?"

"I am the victor after facing Sir Garrett Hudson on the field of honor."

"What?" Dueling meant quite a different thing in Lord Kennington's day. "Did you kill him?"

"No, sir. We fought to first blood. He is merely wounded."

There was more than just a matter of honor involved in these things. No matter the outcome, there would always be a tinge of Scandal of all parties involved. A person who took part in such a deed never wished to be associated with it, no matter the outcome. That was back in *his* day...how things must have changed.

"Well, Lord Kennington? May I have permission to ask Lady Emmeline for her hand?" He showed his lordship the proper respect and address.

"You may address her," said his lordship. If she accepted then they would proceed to the marriage settlements. He had his doubts if this young man would reach that point. His Emmeline was determined and certainly knew her own mind.

"Thank you, my lord." Lord Robert beamed a smile that told of his victory.

This was not how Lord Kennington would have chosen a match for his daughter but if she had given her word, what was he to say?

EMMELINE STROLLED ALONG THE BACK GARDEN WALK ENJOYING THE warm afternoon air and blooming flowers, with her chaperone by her side.

"Where are we to go this evening, Mrs. Peckover?" Em was never tired of dressing in her evening finery and attending parties. For some reason she especially looked forward to the toilette for this evening's party. She felt something extraordinary was about to happen.

"We do not go out tonight, if you will recall, Lord Epping has requested your presence at his party."

"Is that *this* evening?" Em had forgotten. To laugh, dance, and chat with the other guest was all she wished to do—and not with *his* friends. She wanted to meet with hers, Hester, Teresa, and Lucy.

"I don't suppose I could claim a little headache?" Em may not need to pretend. The thought of an entire evening spent with Nicky might bring an actual case of megrims.

"Your mother would be most vexed."

"I suppose she would be." Em could not avoid the obligation.

"Needs must, my dear. Look there, who is that?" Mrs. Peckover motioned toward the house where a man approached.

"I believe that is Lord Robert Blair." His straight, jet-black hair made him easily identifiable.

"The Duke of Ashcroft's son?"

"Exactly." Em was excited to hear what news he brought. She hoped it was good news. Something very exciting, indeed. "I hear he has fought a duel over me this morning."

"A duel!" Mrs. Peckover cried, both shocked and outraged. "How dare he show his face. I daresay there will be a horrible scandal and he will drag you into it."

"Duels are *au courant*, Mrs. Peckover." Em stopped and waited for Lord Robert to reach her.

"Good morning, Lady Emmeline." Lord Robert bowed over her hand. The young, handsome man was out of breath but not from his short walk from the house into the garden.

"And to you, sir," she replied.

"I was wondering if I may speak to you" —Lord Robert glanced from Em to the chaperone— "Privately."

Without a word, Mrs. Peckover gave every indication that she would not take a single step from her charge's side.

"His lordship has given me permission." Lord Robert said the magic words and the chaperone evaporated into the background but was not far away. He once again focused on Em and took up both her hands. "Lady Emmeline, this morning I stood on a dueling field and looked down the barrel of a pistol to win the right for your hand in marriage."

Lord Robert sounded so proper and noble. Em's heart swelled with emotion at the retelling of his brave performance at the duel.

"Only moments ago I met with your father, laying my name, my reputation, and that of my family's for the great honor of asking you to be my wife." He paused and allowed the importance of his words to move her. "Will you marry me?"

Em took a breath. How very romantic this was. Lord Robert's touching marriage proposal was thoughtful and touching indeed.

She wanted that feeling to last. She wanted him to keep saying all those wonderful things to her. His words— Those wonderful sentiments—

"Lady Emmeline?" Lord Robert interrupted her very important thoughts. "Lady Emmeline? Will you marry me?"

She sighed. Alas all those wonderful feelings were soon gone.

"Will you be my wife?"

Em gazed back at Lord Robert. "No, thank you," she replied.

"Excuse me?" He loosened his hold, allowing her hands to slip from his.

"Thank you for asking but.... No, I have no wish to marry you."

"But...I...I thought...." He stopped. Apparently her refusal came as a shock to him. "I duelled for—"

"You are the winner, I take it?"

"Yes, I was...and I imagined as the winner...." His tone softened, losing its warm jubilant quality.

"I do not believe there were any guarantees, my lord." Em told him plainly. "At least none that I gave."

After taking a few moments to contemplate her words he replied, "No, I suppose you did no such thing."

"I am sorry if you thought I might have meant otherwise." Em rewarded him with a smile. "I find you very agreeable and I must say I am happy to see you unharmed."

"Thank you, my lady." Now that Lord Robert calmed, he was much more like his usual self. He glanced about and must have had nothing further to say, and finally.... "I hope you will excuse me. I must take my leave now." He bowed and nearly faltered when taking his first few steps backwards to depart.

"Mr. Winslow, you have returned. *Wonderful!*" Lady Langford welcomed Albert into the entry hall when upon his arrival. He had removed his hat and left it with the butler and kept his gloves, smoothing them over his hands. He still felt self-conscious.

"*Mr. Winslow?*" Frances met him in the foyer and appeared surprised to see him. He heard his name uttered on a gasp, soft on her breath. "*Albert*...what are you doing here?"

Had she not been told to expect his return?

"I'm afraid you must rest the blame for that squarely on your mother's shoulders," he explained. "Her ladyship requested I return this evening to dine with your family. I hope you have no objections, Lady Frances."

"Heavens, no. I am delighted to see you." Sounding a bit distressed, she smoothed the skirts of her frock and turned to her parent. "Why did you not tell me, Mama, I would have worn something" —her voice dropped to a whisper— "*More appropriate.*"

"There is no need, dear," Lady Langford assured her daughter. "This is not a dinner party, only an informal *family* meal. Would you care to be seated in the" —she motioned to the parlor then paused— "But you two had such a lovely time earlier. Perhaps...the weather may not be as warm...." She glanced in the direction of the rear gardens—where he and Frances had spent quite a few memorable hours that morning. "The sun still shines and there is a good hour before we are to be seated."

"Is there enough time for a short stroll?" Frances sounded hopeful. She ran her fingertips over her skirts.

"I daresay there must be. What are you waiting for?" Her ladyship replied with a smile. Lady Langford must have thought them quite thick for it took some time before he and Frances caught on. "Go on...the both of you."

Albert did not need to be asked twice. He did his utmost not to appear too eager and headed down the corridor with Francis not far behind him.

"Wait!" she cried out, bringing them both to a halt.

"What is it?" Albert turned to face her before he reached the door.

Her cheeks were flushed, pink with excitement or exertion. He hoped neither was too much for her.

"Do allow me to fetch Jane's book and we can continue

reading our story just as we discussed this morning." The accompanying smile was quite enchanting.

"What a splendid idea!" With his answer, he believed her intention was to dash back and retrieve the volume herself. "Do send someone for it, if you please. I'd rather you not *run* up and down the staircase."

His request was met with her silent endorsement. She understood well-enough why she should not be traipsing about.

"Is there something you need, my lady?" A footman arrived, he must have heard the commotion.

"Would you please retrieve the small book on my night-stand?" Frances, sounding helpless, accepted that she could not do such a small thing for herself.

"At once." The footman bobbed his head.

"We'll be outside, sitting on the bench at the far end of the garden," she told him before he left down the corridor.

Albert opened the door and waited just outside to escort Frances down the path to said bench. She slid her hand through his arm and rested it in the crook of his elbow before they moved away from the house.

"Perhaps I should have asked for a shawl as well." Frances looked over her shoulder but it was too late for that.

"Do you think the footman could have found it?" Rummaging about in a female's wardrobe was a nightmare.

"Not on his own but he could ask one of the upstairs maids or Saunders, she would know." Frances once again faced forward as they proceeded. "It is of no matter."

Albert had hope if she felt a chill, she might draw closer to him for warmth. The thought caused him to smile. He would welcome a gesture such as that.

"You did not forgo a party to dine here tonight, did you?"

Frances hated to think Albert would give up an evening of merriment and music for a simple family dinner.

"If I wished to attend, I daresay there would be more than enough time after the meal." He smiled at her with genuine warmth and led her down the path toward the bench. "I have a feeling I will find this evening's activities far more enjoyable."

"I have no wish to monopolize your time...." Frances enjoyed his company above all others. "I think we shall have time for another chapter or two of Jane's novel if you like."

"You must not tell a soul that" —he was about to swear her to secrecy— "That...I find that I am *enjoying* this novel. That may not be the case for *all* novels."

"I suppose it is a bit odd for men, isn't it?" She nodded, seemingly understanding. "I shan't breathe a word to anyone."

"It will be our little secret, shall it?"

"Among other things." Just thinking about the free use of their Christian names nearly caused Frances' face to warm. Theirs was not a long acquaintance but familiarity had come quickly. "What will we do after we've finished, Albert?"

"We will ask Miss Stiles for a recommendation." He smiled. "I'm certain she will be more than accommodating."

"I can think of nothing better. It is an excellent idea."

"We can call on her together." He had so easily skipped ahead, planning joint outings they would enjoy. "Perhaps she will have a several in mind and offer us a choice. If she does not possess the books themselves we can always visit the lending library."

"*Call?* You live in the same house as she." The very thought of making these plans as a *couple* gave her pause. Frances was quite flattered that he thought enough of her to intertwine their activities, their time, their *lives*. Mr. Winslow may be over-estimating Frances' ability to travel out and about...even limited travel. For she was not yet allowed outside of the house...only in the back gardens for some fresh air.

"Of course...you will not be calling on *me*. You will be visiting Miss Stiles." The very idea that Frances should be visiting a man would be another scandal! One which she would only have herself to blame.

"That way you are certain to keep your Secret safe."

"Of course you are correct—but I forget, you are in no condition to be paying Morning Calls just yet." Albert must have realized the misstep in his enthusiasm. "But first things first, eh? We have yet to reach the end of this book and then we shall see about going on to the next."

"Yes, you are right." Frances glanced up at him and thought Albert much more handsome than the hero depicted in their story. She then caught the scent of lilac that had drifted on the warm breeze from another part of the garden, reminding her how lovely this moment was.

"We will need to pace ourselves and leave enough for us to read after dinner," he suggested. "If it happens we finish tonight, I can return it to Jane and she could loan you another. And I would be more than happy to deliver it myself on the morrow."

"And we could continue reading the story together?" Frances then began to wonder if it was she or the *novel* in which he had more interest.

"Exactly." He repositioned her hand, drawing her closer. "I would like to take you for a drive in the Park. It may not be much longer for that to happen," Albert supposed. "Something you could do before making Morning Calls, I should think."

"I can hardly wait but there is no need to rush." She was enjoying herself and had no wish to project what she might be doing in a week's time.

"You are so reasonable, *Frances*. It is one of your best qualities."

"Is it?" She never thought of herself as having a *best* quality.

"You have such good common sense. No one can fault you for it. And I believe you are very good at keeping secrets."

"Am I?" That she believed. No one could have grown up in a household with two younger, nosy sisters and not have learned to keep a secret to oneself.

"*Frances*...I do have one other confession...." He came to a halt, stopping both in the center of the garden to disclose this next part.

"Yes?" She gazed at him wondering what more he could disclose to her.

"I am very happy I allowed Kit—*Sir Christopher*...to persuade me to come to London. If I had not, I would not have met you... and that would have been most tragic."

Frances smiled. This was a very nice secret indeed. "I, too, am happy you came to Town."

"I cannot imagine why I had resisted." He stepped forward once again and they were on their way to the bench.

Frances did wish she could have worn something nicer for him. It was well and good that he thought her practical, level-headed, and someone in whom he could confide. She did want him to think she was pretty. He had not said anything that made her believe he saw her as attractive.

"If the dirt should soil the hem of my dress while I am outdoors, I would *need* to change it when we returned to the house," Frances claimed. She felt she needed some excuse to perform a hasty but proper toilette.

"Truly, Francis, there is not a thing wrong with your frock. I find it nice...quite acceptable." He smiled but that was not the reaction for which she wished.

*Acceptable...*how lowering. He must have seen the truth of the matter in her face.

"A different frock could not make you any more marvelous than you are. Please do not do so on my behalf." Albert smiled and held her hand while she sat upon the bench. "If it were up to me, I would not change you one iota."

LATER THAT VERY SAME DAY, LORD KENNINGTON HAD A SECOND visitor into his library, another young man with whom he was not acquainted. Sir Garrett Hudson, as his lordship was to learn, was known more recently as the loser of that morning's duel for the hand of Lady Emmeline. Sir Garrett, bandaged arm and all, entered his lordship's library and bowed.

"Do sit, if you please." Kennington motioned to the chair on the other side of the desk. There was no need to keep him standing. Feeling a bit sympathetic, perhaps his lordship should offer Sir Garrett a bit of Dutch courage, bolster his nerves before embarking on this ramshackle interview that would amount to nothing.

The visitor sat in the very same chair Lord Robert Blair had occupied many hours earlier. Even as the duel's victor, the Duke of Ashcroft's son had not been able to secure Emmeline's heart. His lordship had heard the dismal tale, relayed to him by Mrs. Peckover. Nothing escaped that woman's notice. She was precisely the one needed to oversee his incomprehensible Emmeline.

The earl could not help but feel some sympathy for this poor fellow, he really had been through enough today. He could not know what his lordship already knew, the anticipated result that was yet to come. No matter what this young man did, had done, could do or say would make any difference to Lord Kennington's daughter. Today, Sir Garrett Hudson would be the master of failure.

"It is only a graze, your lordship," Sir Garrett explained. "However, if it should aid in the cause of winning Lady Emmeline, I would gladly welcome my injury."

"Perhaps you can explain something to me, young man." Again, Kennington thought perhaps it was his age or how times had changed...he simply could not see how being involved in a duel, in a possible scandal, should cause him to reap the same benefits of a victor.

"If I can, my lord." Sir Garrett appeared so amiable, it was a shame his day would come to such an unfortunate end. Kennington would wish something better for the young man.

"It is my understanding that you are *not* the victor of the duel...why you are here?"

"Ah...." He shifted in his chair, straightening. "It is highly irregular, I admit, but a few hours ago I learned of Lady Emmeline's refusal of Lord Robert's proposal. At first, I was also perplexed."

Kennington was not surprised at all. This matter was of great confusion to him as well. He would not have expected the loser of the duel to follow in the footsteps of the winner. Hadn't Lord Robert *won* the privilege? Is that not why the duel was fought in the first place? Perhaps the earl misunderstood.

"I imagined her refusal meant it was not her contention that Lord Robert should win. Do you not see? It is *I* she truly wishes to marry." Sir Garrett smiled, very pleased with himself indeed.

Oh. Kennington did not quite see it that way.

"Now that you know why I have asked to speak to you, your lordship. I beg you hear me out."

"I would not dream of interrupting you." Kennington leaned

back in his chair and allowed Sir Garrett to continue. The young man still had to face Emmeline. A refusal of marriage and the muzzle of a pistol might be more than what should be asked of a man in a single day. A weapon had injured his arm, Emmeline might possibly break his heart.

Kennington actually pitied the fellow.

Sir Garrett proceeded to lay out his merits and virtues, his income, and what benefits his lordship's family could gain by connection with his family, whose lineage went back for many generations.

Despite his lordship's opinion that this young man would get no further with his daughter than the first young man. Unless, of course, perhaps Emmeline preferred the loser to the winner. This, his lordship could not know. Lord Kennington gave his permission to pay his address and murmured to himself, "young people" with a shrug as Sir Garrett took his leave.

SEVEN

WHAT WAS MARTIN DOING back at Kennington House? He adjusted the cravat strangling his neck. He could have kicked himself for having to attend this party. There was no reason for him except to provide an escort for his mother and Pauline. This being more of a family obligation than a Society party did not require his presence. He was more than happy to hide in the shadows until he was needed to escort the females of his family for the short journey home.

The main reason Martin did not wish to attend was the possibility that he might run into Epping's sister Emmeline. He strolled down the corridor, going nowhere in particular when he overheard a conversation. Normally he would have continued on but the familiar voice...*voices* caused him to pause outside the door and listen.

"I don't know what to think, Mary." It was Lady Kennington. "His lordship has met with two young men just this afternoon. Each man said that Emmeline was in love with them."

"Both asked for her hand?" Martin recognized his mother as

the second speaker. "What happened? She cannot possibly accept them both."

"They duelled over her this very morning to decide."

This was not news to Martin. They were probably the very same two men he had observed this morning...Lord Robert Blair and the unfortunate Sir Garrett Hudson.

"Can you imagine?" Lady Kennington nearly shrieked. "It's a scandal!"

Martin thought he heard his mother at the start of her swoon. He was not about to give himself away by running into the room to rush to her aid.

"They each asked for Kennington's blessing, which they received from his lordship, and each approached Emmeline, one this morning and one this afternoon. Two offers—and what did she do?"

"Which did she accept?" A third woman, whose voice was unfamiliar to Martin, wanted to know.

"She turned them both away!" Lady Kennington announced.

"Why would she do that?"

"Why, indeed." Lady Kennington had just crossed the line into exasperation. "I cannot imagine what she is playing at. Why does she think she's in Town? I'll tell you why...she is here to find a husband not to play cat and mouse with every fellow she fancies...or does *not* fancy."

"What does Lord Kennington say to this?"

"He thinks she doesn't know her own mind." Lady Kennington sounded as if she had had enough of her daughter.

"Does she, though?" Mrs. Chandler wondered.

"If you ask me, I think we should not allow her to choose because in this instance I believe her mother knows best!"

A man's voice, coming from behind him, said, "Martin, what are you doing here?"

Martin straightened and leapt away from the door. "Just arrived, you know." He was a bit jittery, being caught and all. "I was just...." *Eavesdropping...*but Martin wasn't about to admit that.

"Let's see if we can find something worthwhile to *drink*." Kit passed him in the corridor. "I have a feeling this is going to be a very long night."

Reluctantly, Martin left his spot outside the door, following his friend and glanced over his shoulder, wondering what news he could be missing. Kit was right about finding something substantial to drink. It *was* going to be a long night.

WHAT WAS MARTIN ABOUT...LURKING AROUND AND SUCH IN THE corridor? Christopher had never known his friend to behave in such a havey-cavey manner.

This gathering was meant for a small number of friends—Young Epping, his mates, and some select members of the opposite sex. They were practicing their *savoir faire* by chatting up the females and the young ladies were polishing their flirtation skills on the young men. Christopher supposed both groups needed the practice.

One must acquire Town Bronze and *one* could not do it alone. And it took more than mere observation to acquire the skill. The lot of them seemed to be enjoying themselves in the relatively safe atmosphere of the music room.

"Kit! Kit!" Jane came running in his direction. The fact that she was willing to leave the young men, and her friends, was quite something.

"What is it, poppet?" Christopher gave her his full attention.

"*Epping* has just informed us—"

"That is *Lord* Epping to you," was his gentle reminder. He knew that she knew better than to refer to someone she'd only met recently in such a familiar fashion.

"Yes, Lord Epping has planned...that is...his family...no, Lady Kennington has been so good as to engage Monsieur Philippe for private instruction this evening...just for our little group." The news sent Jane over the moon. She'd been enamored of the *French* dancing master since making his acquaintance last Sunday at Lady Chesney's party.

"Monsieur Philippe expects nothing but the most proper conduct from his pupils."

"Ah, so he won't allow you to refer to Lord Epping by anything except his title."

"That's right." Her tone sounded quite impudent. "If we should need another gentleman to round out our square, rest assured, brother, I shall not suggest that you join us." With that she stalked off, rejoining her friends.

Christopher only hoped her affection for the dancing master went no further than his skill at dance instruction for he did not know what he would do if Jane referred to him as Monsieur *Georges.*

"Martin, you're not keeping watch over Pauline as you should." Christopher leaned against the archway between the conservatory and the music room. He kept watch on Jane, ready to step in at the first sign of impropriety. "Jane's just told me Lady Kennington has invited Monsieur Philippe to provide private dance instruction this evening."

Martin looked up at this. "Is that that fellow from Lady Chesney's do? The one whom Pauline and Jane could not stop talking about?"

"The very same." Christopher sensed that Martin was of like

mind, both uncertain of the fellow. "I can't say I'm happy about it. There was something not quite right about him."

It was Christopher's opinion that the Frenchman, if he was indeed a Frenchman, seems somewhat at odds with his manner and the way he spoke.

A commotion, one that only occurred with young people who had learned manners but not as of yet put them into practice, announced that the much anticipated dancing master had arrived. The din was enough to alert Martin, returning him to Christopher's side to observe the goings-on for himself.

The newly arrived visitor, tall and lean, Monsieur Philippe in *au courant* fashion had made his appearance. A second gentleman followed, carrying a bulging leather folder in his arms. Monsieur Philippe appeared elegant in a splendidly tailored Imperial Blue colored jacket. The white of his waistcoat, matching white breeches, stockings, and dancing slippers, creating an uninterrupted line down his long limbs and he sketched a bow. The assistant inclined his head.

The dancing master gestured to the pianoforte and the assistant scurried to the instrument, opened his folder, and arranged his music.

"As I said, there is no need for an orchestra, we are here merely to learn." He spoke unlike any Frenchman Christopher had heard speaking English—not posh English but not from the country.

Monsieur Philippe welcomed his admirers, greeting them accordingly, acting with proper humility when the guests had remembered him. Every gesture he made had an elegance and grace befitting his profession. The side panels of his brocade coat appeared to be cut on the longish side and swirled about him almost like a cape. It flared from his body as he pivoted from side to side. The man was a walking embodiment of what a dancing master should be, at least, how he should appear.

Where had he come by such a garment, Christopher wondered. Not made in England, surely. He had never seen anything of similar construction. Bespoke, certainly...perhaps made in Paris? That was the popular consensus regarding the dancing master's origin...according to Jane and Pauline.

"Bit plain, ain't he?" Christopher remarked, not at all jealous. He'd admired the cut and fit of the man's clothing but the pigment...actually the *lack* of pigment.

"What's that?"

"All in white except for his jacket. It's a bit plain." He simply did not approve, rather, it was not to his taste.

Martin glanced down at Christopher's chest. "You're one to talk. What happened to your...your...." He gestured at his cream-colored waistcoat with its simple embroidered embellishment along the exposed edges.

"Jane made me promise not to wear one of my new creations. She didn't want me showing up the young men."

"And distracting them from the young ladies," Martin quipped. "You must admit Kit, there is a danger in that."

Christopher did not react and focused his attention on the group, never taking his eyes from the group.

"As long as you're watching Jane, you can keep an eye on Pauline, can't you?" Martin must have been feeling grumpy and not in a mood to tolerate any sort of nonsense from the younger folk.

"The music room is so vast, I cannot keep watch of the entire room alone."

"You are more than capable. Do not underestimate yourself, my friend." Martin knew just how cavernous it was. He'd spent many an hour pacing the length of that room. This evening, he was confined to the conservatory.

Monsieur Philippe started the group in several long lines, each learning the steps of their dance. Then they were paired with partners, then placed together in small groups to practice. A good hour had passed and all the guests finally arrived and the dancing could begin in earnest.

This was a lack-luster affair. Martin could have easily fallen asleep while Kit remained alert, stationed at the archway.

Lo and behold, Lady Emmeline made her entrance.

"*Good evening....*" Kit crooned, alerting Martin that something had finally happened.

He moved across the room to peer over his friend's shoulder. "Gracious, talk about causing a stir."

Emmeline wore a simple cream-colored gown with a dotted overskirt of palest yellow, giving her an ethereal presence, and she glided into the music room. She gave the appearance of an angel.

No doubt every young lady felt inadequate, completely outshined by the more sophisticated Season's Incomparable.

With Lady Emmeline, an experienced dance partner, by his side, Monsieur Philippe could now properly demonstrate the steps accompanied by music, to the delight of the roomful of attentive pupils. Lady Kennington stood nearby assuring the cooperation of her daughter.

After the demonstration, a good half hour in length, was complete Emmeline received a well-earned appreciation from the instructor and guests and was allowed to leave the gathering.

With a "*Merci, Mademoiselle,*" from Monsieur Philippe, she curtsied to the dancing master and wished the guests a pleasant 'Good Evening' without inquiring if she should return.

If he were a betting man Martin would have placed a monkey on the lady avoiding such an occurrence.

She walked through the music room and toward the adjacent conservatory. It was unknown to Martin if she knew it was where he and Kit had hidden to keep out of the way.

"Good evening, gentlemen," Emmeline finally spoke, realizing there were others in the room.

"Lady Emmeline," Kit returned. Martin simply nodded and said nothing.

She entered the conservatory and passed both men, continuing to the far end of the room. "You must feel this gathering is tedious, do you not?" Was she reflecting her own emotions on to them?

"It is tolerable," Kit replied.

"They are far too young for this. Young men at eighteen and young ladies at sixteen are not suited to socialize together." She apparently did not approve despite her parents' willingness to support her brother's request for this party.

Martin wanted to say something. He should, apparently Emmeline's parents were too weak to stand up to their daughter and deliver a proper set-down. It was not her place to voice an opinion and her personal feelings on the matter were irrelevant.

"Martin?" Kit called over his shoulder. "Is Pauline stepping out of line here? I don't mean *literally,* of course...do you think I should intervene?"

Martin moved to his right to peer past Kit into the music room.

"She's fine, Kit." Martin returned to his original position away from the archway. "Pauline is doing nothing more than occupying herself while waiting her turn, the same as Jane."

"I don't care for it at all, Martin." Kit never took his eyes from their sisters. "They're much too young to gad about with young men like this."

The *I-told-you-so* expression Emmeline wore was nearly too much for him to bear and the accompanying shrug was intolerable.

"They are only learning to dance!" Martin bellowed. "For Heaven's Sake, Kit, stop being such a *dashed* Mother Hen! If they are in need of supervision send for—Mrs. Heffel-*ling*— Heffel-*white*— *Heffelfinger!*"

With that outburst, Kit lifted a chair—rather loudly, and placed it right at the archway of the music room with a tooth-jarring bang. There, he could watch every movement, and sat with great elan, giving a loud grunt of dissatisfaction at what he thought of Martin's outburst.

A tea tray arrived and set close to Kit, at his insistence. He continued to ignore the others in the room, creating a watch-tower from where he could safely observe the social gaiety, watching for improprieties.

Martin did not appreciate his friend leaving him with the hostess' daughter. Kit had not physically left but his attention was now fully focused on the activity in the other room while Martin shared the remainder of the conservatory with Emmeline. She was responsible for his current bought of the blue-devils, and he wasn't particularly good about restraining his temper.

"I've heard that you received two marriage proposals today." Martin spoke as nonchalantly as if he were conversing about something as insignificant as the weather.

"Yes, I did," she replied. Emmeline did not move and continued to gaze out the window, displaying her profile to him.

"And you refused them both." He continued with a bit more irritation.

"Yes, I did." Still she showed no emotion. No remorse. No regret.

Had she not understood what she had done? Had she not understood what she had put those men through? Had she really *no* idea?

Martin glanced over his shoulder at his friend and approached Emmeline to address her directly, hoping to keep this dialogue private although Kit sat twenty or so feet away.

"You have done those two men a grave injustice. They have both professed love for you, so much so they met on the dueling field over your affections which, in your callousness, you have denied both men."

"It is my decision to make, is it not?" She met his eyes and spoke with some venom.

"It is not your right to ruin their lives." Martin felt completely justified in bringing this to her attention. "I have watched you over these last few days and can quite honestly say that you are a shameless flirt!"

Emmeline stamped her foot with a huff.

"You encouraged those men to fight for your affections," he chided her.

"I most certainly did not. *Rude!*" she uttered under her breath. "They took it upon themselves thinking to impress me by doing so."

"And did it impress you?" Her answer did not come and Martin suspected it had but she did not wish to say it out loud. "I heard them on the field—'*For the hand of Lady Emmeline Cordia-Darling!*'"

"Did they really?" she uttered softly, then smiled.

"Do you not realize that they could have killed each other?" Martin stressed in quiet outrage. "You simply cannot turn men against one another on a whim."

"No one was hurt," she said, her voice meek. Had he detected a bit of repentance? "It was rather exciting, really...to have two men fight over you."

"*Exciting?*" Martin could hardly believe it. How could she think it was of such little consequence? "If one of them had been killed.... I shudder to think of what could have happened."

Emmeline's expression faded and she interlaced her fingers, then pressed her hands tightly together. It was the first indication he'd seen that the idea of one of them dying had suddenly occurred to her.

"You are better than that," he whispered, as if he could will her to alter the way she viewed her behavior. "You *must* be better than that. How can someone as clever as you, who has such insight regarding other people and the ability to befriend nearly anyone not benefit by those gifts?"

"You think I have *gifts*?" Emmeline's once dark expression began to lighten.

"When you came to Town, every young lady who met you wanted to be your friend and there wasn't a gentleman who was not captivated by your charm and beauty. I've heard you referred to as the Season's Incomparable."

Emmeline blushed at the compliment but his words were not meant to please her. He was just relaying facts as he understood them. Martin recalled the day he first set eyes on her after not seeing her for nearly a decade...beautiful and alluring. A few moments later, she would demonstrate quite a different aspect... naughty and mischievous.

"I recall, it was just over a fortnight ago, you came to the house to meet Pauline and Jane for a shopping expedition. I believe you and your mother arrived late."

"I was not late," she denied, sounding offended.

"You were the last to arrive by quite some time." His arched eyebrow quelled any further impertinence on her part.

"Only by a few minutes, perhaps."

"I cannot say why you resorted to such a churlish thing…it might have been that you were feeling a bit left out because you were not included in the conversation and laughter inside the parlor with the others. Perhaps you saw an opportunity you could not pass. For whatever reason, you took Pauline's glove and hid it."

"What? I did not!" Her indignation was much air and bluster.

"I saw you do so myself." Martin smiled. She could deny the act all she wanted, he knew it to be true. "It wasn't a terribly cruel trick but an *impish* one."

"An imp? Me?" Emmeline stomped her foot and clearly whispered, "*Rude!*"

"I admit that was a harmless prank. No one was hurt by it." Martin did not think that, by itself, made Emmeline a monster but his tale was not complete.

"I thought their confusion would be funny. Jane and Pauline searched for it and when they found it they laughed. It was such a lark!"

"I saw you for the second time at the Venetian Breakfast and a third time, some hours later the very same day. The young woman with whom I drove through Hyde Park wasn't particularly agreeable. She did not care for my company, nor did I care for hers. We shan't speak of Lady Charlotte's ball, shall we?"

This garnered a wordless but not silent outburst. Her small, slippered foot assailed the carpet again.

"I had the misfortune of seeing this very same young lady at the Everett party just last night. It was then I realized you had changed. You were not the same young lady who thought a misplaced glove amusing, you had progress from fun to some-thing more dangerous...setting man against man, suitor against suitor."

"I don't know what you're talking about," she refuted. Martin knew it to be a lie. He was there from the beginning and had seen it all.

"I watched as she flirted quietly and with great skill during a country dance with Sir Garrett Hudson to only plead with Lord Robert that he should do what he could to prove his affection for her an hour later." Martin felt the tightness in his jaw as he recalled and retold the events.

Emmeline made no sound.

"It would not surprise me to learn that *she* is friend to no one. After today I don't know that anyone would want to share her company."

She closed her eyes. Was she pretending he was not there, and if he was not there she could not hear what he had to say.

"Oh, *Em-me-line*." Martin shook his head in exasperation? In shame? In pity? How could she have evolved into such a contemptible callous creature? "Is that who you are now? Is that what you've become?"

He could see her eyes fill with tears. She may not have let on that his words had an affect but clearly they had. This honest display of herself, of how she appeared to others, was long overdue.

Why had someone not said something to her before now? Why was it up to Martin to bring her to task, she was nothing to him...except a continual thorn in his side that for some unknown reason that caused him such irritation.

"What do your friends say when you steal away with their beaus only later to cast them aside? And now there are gentlemen who risked their lives, who then asked you to be their wife and you refused them. What will it be next?"

"But I'm not interested in marrying any of them." There may have been a tremor in her words, and a hint of a sob.

"Then why bother to encourage them? This is not a sport. The entire purpose of attending the Season is for men and women, young and old, to make a suitable match." He did not know if his words were making any sense to her. She didn't look at him. She didn't— "You are the most meddlesome managing minx!" Martin enunciated each word so she would clearly hear his insult. Her aloofness infuriated him, then he finally had a reaction.

"*Rude!*" Emmeline stamped her foot showing her full displeasure at his opinion, and with a dramatic huff, strode out of the room.

Martin walked in the opposite direction to where Kit sat, not so far away that he could not have heard every word. He stared deeply into his teacup as if it were the most interesting thing in the world.

"Just stirring the sugar in," Kit murmured.

"What are you talking about?" Martin pulled over a chair, dragging it along the carpet before dropping into the seat in his own pique and grumbled. "You don't even take sugar in your tea."

eight

MEDDLESOME! MANAGING! MINX!

That *hateful* man! Em was so very vexed she could not see straight. She dare not lose her temper with so many people about. It would not have been a shock to find she had frightened the guests with her violent, physical outburst as she stomped down the corridor and up the stairs, heading for her bedchamber.

Meddlesome! Managing! Minx!

How *dare* he—that...*that man* call her those names. How *dare* he!

Martin Chandler...merely thinking his very name made Em want to—want to— She wasn't certain what it was she wished to do but it was not something pleasant.

Yell, or throw something, or just plain scream! Emmeline slammed her bedchamber door behind her and stalked to the window to glare outside.

How could he say she ruined someone's life? She had done no such thing. Lord Robert and Sir Garrett acted freely. She could not deny she found it secretly thrilling to hear they were fighting over her affections. But that she had tricked or coerced them into doing so, it was nothing of the sort.

For Martin to say that she purposely misdirected her friends.... Em had told various friends she cared for one man and certain other friends she cared for someone else, that was not done with malice in mind. It was told to the only as a joke, just as a jest.

She had not stolen anyone's beau nor had she dissuaded any man from following his heart.

Well...not on purpose, really.

No. Martin was wrong. And he...he made her feel awful.

Em had no wish for anyone to die...especially in a duel over her. Thinking on that for a few minutes...it would have been dreadful if something had happened to either Lord Robert or Sir Garrett.

What they must have gone through...how could she have allowed it? Although she hadn't exactly encouraged the duel, Em did nothing to try and stop it.

And to top it off the winner, Lord Robert, tried to claim his reward, Em's favor. She had known it would ultimately be to ask for her hand in marriage. To be completely honest she had no interest in him in the first place. Had she broken his heart? No, they did not know one another well enough for that. Recalling his expression when she refused him.... Em may not have broken his heart but he had been shocked by her answer. Now that she thought about it...she felt quite ashamed.

Poor Sir Garrett...the loser of the duel. He literally had been wounded, shot in the arm. After learning Lord Robert's offer had been refused the baronet convinced himself that Em's true affection lay with him and not Lord Robert. That was not the case, Sir Garrett was wrong, and Em had refused his offer as well.

Em had displayed very poor judgement and behaved very

badly. She realized that now. She should have never allowed that situation to get out of hand. Maybe Martin was right. She was a *meddlesome managing minx.*

No one had ever addressed her in that manner. How did he know about those small indiscretions she'd taken? And she wondered if he had known *everything.*

How could he have seen her hide Pauline's glove? Surely she would have seen him. It vexed her. He had taken it upon himself to act as her conscious. She didn't care for it, and she cared for it even less because he might be right and she never wanted to admit that.

Em believed she was a better person than *he* thought she was...as if *his* opinion would ever matter to her. She had no need to please him but she did wish to prove to herself that she was, indeed, a better person than he made her out to be.

She felt sorry for the gentlemen she refused earlier. She felt ill at ease for the friends she misled...for deceived was too harsh a term because she had thought of it as some amusement...all in good fun...it had started out that way.

Martin Chandler had made her see the situation differently. Then Emmeline realized she needed to do something and set things to right. That's what she needed to do.

The bigger question would be, was it even possible for her to make amends?

"LOOK WHO HAS COME TO VISIT!" LADY LANGFORD'S VOICE HELD such jubilance when she came upon Albert just as he stepped into the foyer of Langford House that next morning.

"As a frequent guest, it warms my heart that my arrival can still elicit such excitement from you, my lady." Albert rested his gloved hand upon his chest and bowed. He thought her reaction quite funny.

"You must know we were not expecting you until much later. It is a good thing you have arrived when you have."

"Is it? I am only too happy to accommodate you."

"Oh, you silly man, come inside, will you?" She waved him into the front parlor and turned to the butler, "Do send a maid to Frances' room and fetch her, will you? Tell her Mr. Winslow awaits."

Albert stepped inside the front parlor and waited for Lady Langford before being seated. She sat in a chair while he took a seat on one side of the sofa, nearest to her.

"Before Frances joins us, may I ask your opinion of her progress?"

"I am no physician, ma'am. My opinion hardly matters."

"If you do not know, then who?" She gave him a knowing look. "You spend a great deal of time with her, have you not formed an opinion as to whether she is ready to step out into society?"

"Do you think she is ready?" Albert had anticipated the day this would happen but had not expected the time to come so soon.

"I ask only because an opportunity has arisen." She watched his reaction to her proposal. "Lady Barrington is a great friend of mine. I accepted her invitation weeks ago. I had nearly forgotten with our recent crisis that came upon us. Now that has been resolved, I have no wish to cry off now."

Albert understood that she wished to honor her commitment to her friend. But to bring Frances along.... Was she ready? Did she wish to attend? He wasn't certain and did not think he was the one to make that determination.

"I had thought we could just drop in and stay but a moment.

What say you, sir?" Lady Langford stared at Albert. "I can think of no one better to accompany us, that is, Frances and I, to Lady Barrington's this evening."

"This evening?" Albert thought this all rather sudden. However, if he were to accompany them. He would be on hand to see to Frances' comfort and safely delivered home.

"I am of two minds about this." She shook her head, still wrestling with indecision. "Your input on this matter would be of value to me."

Frances appeared at the doorway and Albert stood.

"Do come in, my dear," Lady Langford called to her daughter.

"It is very good to see you," Frances smiled and held her hand out to him. He accepted her hand, placing his gloved fingertips under her palm and bowed.

"This is unexpected...." She held his gaze while making her way to the opposite end of the sofa from him and sat nearest her mother. Albert retook his seat.

"I have returned Miss Stiles' book to her and...." Albert could not say what he treasured most about Frances at that very moment. The pleasant sound of her voice? Was it the sparkle in her eyes as she held his gaze. He did not wish to share *their* enjoyment of Jane's novel with Lady Langford. It was a particular diversion they only shared together. "It seems at a most fortuitous time because your mother has asked me to accompany you to Lady Barrington's party this evening."

"If you are a willing participant, Mr. Winslow, and would be so good as to accompany us, then I would be delighted to attend, Mama."

"Excellent!" Lady Langford stood, happy with her daughter's response. Albert immediately took to his feet. "I have every confidence you shan't allow Frances to become overly tired. All I ask is that you arrive at a decent hour and do not allow us to remain above two hours."

So much for *staying for a few minutes*.... Albert would never allow Frances to become overtired and agreed to Lady Langford's terms. She soon left the two to discuss the reason for his visit.

"I have completed the errand," Albert told Frances in a soft voice, he did not wish to be overheard by her ladyship.

"Did you tell Jane how entertaining we are finding the story?" Frances must send a note telling Cousin Jane just how delighted they were with her choice.

"I told her how much *you* were enjoying it." Apparently, he wasn't quite ready to make his secret known beyond the confines of this room.

Frances understood his reticence. Not many men read, much less enjoyed, novels.

"And she has sent to you...." He drew out a small book from the inside of his jacket.

"You've brought another! That is wonderful! Thank you so much, Albert." Frances took the small book from him and did what he could not do...open the cover and turn to the Title page...*Volume 2*. She was very glad there would be no interruption in the story!

"Don't thank me, thank Jane. She is happy you find the story amusing and is very glad to loan you the subsequent volumes." Frances knew he was just as pleased as she about having possession of the next book. The tale would continue for both of them!

"But you're the one who has brought it." Of course Frances was delighted to see Albert. In truth, she was getting used to having him around, and the day his visits ended would be sad indeed. He took her for walks, joked with her, and kept her company in general. It was kind of him to act as an intermediary. It made the process so much quicker.

"True. She's already finished and was very happy to pass it on to you."

"Shall we start it now?" Frances gazed at him wide-eyed, hoping he would agree.

"What about your breakfast...you have only just come from your bedchamber, you must be famished."

"What is *food* when we have a story to read?" Frances did not wait for him to offer his arm. She fairly grabbed him by the elbow and started toward the back of the house to the rear gardens. "Let us retreat to our bench while it is still light and the weather pleasant. I'm certain we can read at least two chapters before our absence is discovered."

nine

IT WAS JUST AFTER ten in the morning before Emmeline ventured belowstairs. She did not sleep well last night, after Nicky's party. What sleep she managed was filled with nightmares. Dreams of being alone, abandonment, and enduring social torture kept her slumber from restful. There was nothing for it but to rise early, far too early for even her lady's maid to attend her.

Still in her wrapper, Em descended the staircase. The drapes stood open filling the rooms with crisp morning light. Gone were the floral tributes that once lined the walls. The rooms were becoming empty and Em was alone. She didn't care for this. She wanted the gaiety and laughter from her groups of friends to return.

Would there be new ones to take their place? Would there ever be? At this moment Em doubted it. She had felt the adoration and acceptance when she looked at the flowers surrounding her in previous days. Now their numbers dwindled, removed as the older ones wilted and faded and none arrived to take their place. It did not speak well for her reputation.

Her fear of abandonment might come true and it would be all her fault. Last night she promised herself that she would make amends to those she had wronged. Today, she needed to plan how that would happen.

What was she going to do? She wasn't sure. Where would she turn? Where was she even to begin? And who would be the ones to benefit? Those she had wronged of course but she was unsure with whom she should start. She did wish there was someone to advise her.

Em still had her friends, perhaps some of them, if they would have her, and a few social commitments that remained. She would make the most of them. Hopefully, it would be enough.

"HOW IS IT THAT YOU ACCOMPANY BOTH JANE *AND* PAULINE shopping this morning?" Mrs. Heffelfinger walked alongside Christopher down Bond Street behind the young girls. "Since when do you willingly take responsibility for Miss Chandler?"

"I am loathe to admit it" —Christopher did not wish to utter the words— "Because it is for purely selfish reasons."

"Really?" Mrs. Heffelfinger had a questioning tone in her voice, surprised at his interest in the young miss.

"Jane is my dearest sister but I find her exhausting at times... most of the time. I am an inadequate replacement for a female friend. Including Miss Chandler in our outings relieves me of having to suffer Jane's need for attention." Christopher swung his walking stick forward as he strolled along. "She is better at occupying Jane's time than I. As I said, Mrs. H, my actions are not as charitable as one might believe."

"We need to pay Cousin Frances a call," Jane informed her brother over her shoulder. "It's been an age."

"Poor thing, she's been locked away in her house since her return, and she's had nothing to do." Pauline sounded equally sympathetic.

"She has finished the book I left her last we were there."

"Has she? Did she enjoy it?"

"She's asked for the second volume. *Albert* was good enough to bring it to her." Jane widened her eyes, staring at Pauline.

"Oh...you mean *Al-bee*," Pauline drew it out. She knew very well Christopher did not approve of her use of *Albee*. It was improper and far too familiar. Both young ladies giggled.

"I must confess that there is a price to pay when the two are brought together," Christopher said to Mrs. Heffelfinger but loud enough for all to hear. Then he cleared his throat. "Sometimes it is my blushes."

The young ladies, who had obviously been eavesdropping, broke into laughter once again.

"Oh, that's just female-talk they go on about, you know. They don't mean it." Mrs. Heffelfinger, whose time as a girl must have been a very long time ago, seemed to remember quite well.

"Yes, I'm afraid I do understand. These two have no mercy. It happens to be more than just my pride that is injured." Christopher resented his hat upon his head, hoping that would alleviate his growing discomfort. "I believe, monetarily speaking, this stroll down Bond Street will lighten my purse considerably by the acquisition of two bonnets—if I am lucky."

"*Two*—Sir Christopher?" Mrs. Heffelfinger turned to her left to glare at him in feigned shock. "I am sure you are quite mistaken." She fluttered her lashes, graced him with a gentle smile, and softened her voice to correct him, "I am sure you mean *three*."

EMMELINE STEPPED INSIDE THE BARRINGTON RESIDENCE, HER mother left to find the hostess while Mrs. Peckover remained by her side. Em adjusted her gloves, pulling them tight to fit around her fingers, and pushed them below her elbow as was the fashion. She could not forget the words Martin Chandler spoke last night.... *I don't know that anyone would want to share your company.*

For the present, it seemed to be true. No one greeted her and she still stood alone. This had never happened to her. Where were her friends, acquaintances, and admirers?

She could not shed the feeling of personal disgrace...of her unforgivable behavior...and she had no one else to blame but herself. If this was not a public scandal, it certainly was a private one. Again his words haunted her.... *You are the most meddlesome managing minx!*

Last night, her grand plan to redeem herself seemed feasible, currently it seemed an impossible dream, fraught with difficulty. Where would she begin?

She wasn't certain if anyone would acknowledge her much less speak to her. How would she return to the good graces of her previous acquaintances when she would not be received? Perhaps her social standing was worse than she had feared. Perhaps she would find herself *persona non grata*.

Em need not be concerned with her appearance. She took great pains with her toilette, making certain she did her utmost to appear at her best. She entered the ballroom dressed in the prerequisite white gown, trimmed with pale-colored silk flowers. In addition, she had fresh blossoms placed in her hair. Alas, there was one here to compliment her upswept tresses. No one here to applaud her gown. No one here to admire her.

She kept watch for any odd, unwanted stares leveled her way when stepping into the ballroom. There were groups of people but she did not find the animosity she thought she might encounter. All were civil and greeted her openly but no longer welcoming, wanting to keep her company, nor was she beseeched with requests for dances, as was the norm.

"How very sad you look, Emmeline." Lady Amelia Luce approached, sounding somewhat concerned and sympathetic.

"Amelia! Good evening!" Em smiled, happy to see a friend. Mrs. Peckover stepped back, not abandoning her but made herself less visible with the arrival of Amelia. "You look quite lovely tonight."

"Thank you." Amelia, quite possibly inspired by Emmeline, had adopted the gold trim alteration to her plain white gown, transforming it nicely. "You are a vision—a flower garden come to life. The blooms in your hair smell heavenly."

"You are too kind, Amelia." Em had no wish to reveal her true mood, only wishing to appear as animated and jubilant as if nothing in the world were wrong and she had not a care. "I may have spent too long on my toilette and afraid I may be a tad late."

"Nonsense," Amelia returned just as playfully as ever. "The party has yet begun. Emmeline" —her friend stepped closer— "I must say that it is very brave of you to attend."

"Need I be brave?" Em had no idea exactly what she would meet up with but expected she would soon learn.

"I'm afraid you will not find you are as welcome as you once were." Amelia's voice softened as she delivered the regrettable news.

"I suppose that is what happens when one has brought

about scandal in one's life." There was no one else to blame and Em knew that. "Am I thoroughly despised?"

"I do not think your reputation has sunk that far."

"I did so wish to redeem myself. Do you think it possible? Have I a chance, Amelia?"

"I don't think I can answer that." Of course if it were up to kind-hearted Amelia, Em would be forgiven in a thrice. "It depends on what you have done and what you want to do to correct people's opinions." Amelia seemed to very much have the upper hand on Em. Her direct stare begged Em to confide in her. "Did you refuse Lord Robert's marriage proposal after he won the duel for your hand?"

"Amelia...I never promised anyone I would accept a marriage proposal based on the outcome of a duel. You should know me better than that." To choose a husband in such a manner would be beyond foolish. That would leave the entire decision, one Em held very close to her heart, up to mere chance.

"Then I heard Sir Garrett had approached you as well." Amelia shook her head. "He lost the duel. How are such things possible?"

"I cannot say I *understand* the rules of dueling and what is acceptable. But Sir Garrett did seek me out some hours after I refused Lord Robert. It all happened very quickly, really. It was entirely unexpected. Of course, I said No."

"*That,* I completely understand." Amelia glanced around and must have noticed the very same as Em had herself. During the time the two conversed, no one approached to renew their acquaintance with the once very popular earl's daughter.

Em felt it...the weight of her wrongdoing. Now she paid the price. Emmeline was a social outcast.

ten

LADY FRANCES ABBOTT ENTERED the Barrington residence on the arm of Albert Winslow. It was, after all, Frances' first foray beyond the confines of her family's home and she should not, as her mother put it...*over do*. Lady Langford suggested they should stroll about until her return.

She would be but a moment.

Frances could not think how that could be possible. Locating Lady Barrington would take a great effort itself for the house was large, the rooms were many, and the persons milling about were plentiful. However, Frances would not mind. The view was different from that of her rear gardens and the most important person in her life at the moment stood beside her. Albert.

Readjusting her gloved hand, she moved it beneath his own gloved one. He trapped her hand in a secure yet gentle hold. She felt quite safe when with him.

"Do you know I believe you are the loveliest young lady in the room," Albert whispered into her ear.

She felt the flush of warmth in her cheeks at his words. "You cannot know that, you have yet to step into the ballroom where I daresay there will be many more ladies who may appeal you."

"I am afraid I must disagree," he replied. "I am quite partial to only one."

"That is very kind of you to say." Frances recalled how they discussed attending a party together and how they spoke of their wanting to share a dance. This could not be what Albert wanted nor was it what she had envisioned. "I cannot dance this evening. I know you had wished to—"

"We are not here to dance, merely to attend, by your mother's request," he reminded her. "It is for her benefit that we attend not ours. Do not concern yourself, we will have our dance when the time comes. Let us proceed, shall we?"

Albert was kind enough to allow her to choose which direction Frances wished to walk. Meaning, if she was stationed on his right, she might bump into those standing about in the room. If she were positioned to his left, she would have the safety of the walls of the room on one side and the protection of his body on her right. She preferred the latter.

Walking with her back slightly angled toward the wall gave Frances the opportunity, while speaking to Albert, to glance at the guests without having to interact with them. Actually, there were very few who looked remotely familiar. Until....

"Is that Lady Emmeline?" Frances thought she glimpsed a familiar face from nearly across the room. Albert stopped and had a look for himself.

"I have had the pleasure of an introduction but having seen her only once, I cannot be certain."

"It is!" Frances felt as if it had been a very long time since she'd seen her friend. Lady Emmeline's face brightened when she turned toward Frances and recognition struck her as well. "May we meet with her, please?"

"Of course. If that is what you wish." Albert altered their path and moved in Lady Emmeline's direction.

Frances and Emmeline rushed toward the other with outstretched arms.

"I had no idea you were to attend," Emmeline blurted out in a rush.

"I had no idea I *was* attending until this afternoon," Frances honestly answered. "I should have known you would be here."

Emmeline motioned to the young lady standing by her side. "Are you acquainted with—"

"Yes, of course. Lady Amelia, it is good to see you again." Frances nodded. It had been quite a while but she remembered the introduction, made by Emmeline, at a previous gathering albeit it had been some time ago.

"Is this...." Emmeline glanced at Albert. She clearly understood they had arrived together.

"Mr. Winslow. He says you two have previously met," Frances recited what Albert had told her earlier.

"So we have." Emmeline dipped into a curtsy, as did Lady Amelia.

"Mr. Winslow...I do recall but it has been some time go," Lady Amelia recalled. "Last month perhaps."

"I believe you are correct." Albert bowed to both ladies. "Still, I am pleased to see you once again."

"Lady Barrington and my mother are friends." Frances explained. "We accompanied her this evening to make an appearance at her ladyship's house party."

"She is friends with my mother as well." Emmeline laughed. "It seems Lady Barrington is acquainted with many members of the *ton*."

"Goodness...is that Sir Christopher?" Lady Amelia's comment did not go unnoticed. While the young ladies only took a mild interest in his presence, to Albert, his friend's appearance held some serious significance.

"He must have just arrived and I would like a word with him." Albert gazed at Frances. "Would you mind if I excused myself for a few minutes?"

"Have no fear, Mr. Winslow," Frances reassured him. "I will remain with Lady Amelia, Lady Emmeline, and Mrs. Peckover until you return. I feel I shall be quite safe in their company."

"Very well." He nodded to the ladies and departed.

"That man does worry so. This is London. Nothing will befall you in the middle of a crowded ballroom," Amelia declared as if Frances' abduction was not known to her.

Perhaps it was not.

"Oh, goodness...." Frances quickly cast her gaze to the floor. "Just my luck! The very first party I attended in more than a fortnight and I run into *him*." She turned away from Em, clearly hiding her face from recognition.

"Is it someone you wish to avoid?" Of course Em knew first hand how it was like not to want to draw attention from a particular gentleman, but she could deal with it far more efficiently than Frances.

"It is Mr. Gilbert. I made his acquaintance sometime ago and we shared a county dance. It was during one of my first balls. He sent flowers the very next morning and paid me a call the next day."

"That is expected," Amelia remarked, but must not have understood Frances' aversion to the man. On second thought, *aversion* was quite a strong word. Perhaps she ought to have said *off-putting*.

"I am sorry but there is something about him that does not sit right with me." Frances really could not explain, one could sense the discomfort she must have felt while she spoke about this. "He is a kind soul but to tell you true, he is a bit odd. He did not seem all that interested in courting. He apologized, saying if he seemed forward but his mother had insisted he send the flowers and pay his respects."

"Whyever would he apologize? Had you offended him in some way?" Em was very curious about this peculiar man. "That's not like you at all, Frances."

"That is what he said. I dreaded he might offer to take me on a drive but he said he could not because the faintest whiff of horse would cause him to sneeze."

"Goodness!" Amelia drew back. "It is a wonder how he can manage to get around Town."

"He says he walks."

"There is only so far one can walk, you know." The idea did not appeal.

"According to Mr. Gilbert, closed carriages are quite tolerable during long journeys."

"I see. How nice that is for him." Amelia held back her laughter but a few snickers escaped.

"Yes, I thought so too." Frances continued her story, "He refused a stroll to nearby Grosvenor Square or to walk in our back garden."

"Whatever is wrong with your back garden?" Amelia could not help herself but inquire.

"It has grasses," Frances replied. "He informed me that *all* grasses make his eyes water profusely and burn."

"Gracious! I have never heard of such— The man does sound like a *quiz*."

"However, he did suggest that we could meet at the lending library if I would like."

"The lending library?" This sent Amelia into a further bout of hysterics.

All of a sudden, Em felt her eyes widen as she was struck with some inspiration. Frances did not know what had come over her friend. It was a bit concerning.

"Emmeline, are you quite all right?" Frances took Em's hand. "You look a bit flushed."

And she felt a bit breathless as inspiration struck.

Em grasped on to Frances' hand in return and drew her near. "Would you do me a great favor and make Mr. Gilbert known to me?"

"Emmeline, really! After all I've told you?" Frances reeled in disbelief.

Lady Frances might not believe Em would hold the slightest bit of interest in Mr. Hugh Gilbert.

On the contrary, she had.

"I shall if you insist." Frances turned her face into the crowd and when she saw him...Mr. Gilbert, she smiled and, as Emmeline had requested, encouraged him to approach.

IT WAS A MISTAKE FOR HIM TO LEAVE FRANCES. ALBERT HAD FELT uneasy about it but he wouldn't be absent long. He felt she could be left in the small group for a few minutes while he had a word with Kit. But Albert had a swift change of mind once he'd reached the halfway point between the two.

With a glance back, Albert was distressed when observing a man joining the ladies whom he just left. Where had Lady Amelia gone? *Safe....* He thought Frances would be protected while in their company. Albert felt her safety was compromised now that only two remained by Frances' side. Why did Lady Emmeline's chaperone not step in and shield them from the intruder?

"Speaking to another gentleman is not cause to become outraged in public, Albee." Kit had cut to the heart of the matter. "Frances shows no sign of distress. She is perfectly fine with her female friends."

That was not the type of greeting he'd expected from his friend. "How did you know I was—"

"I can see it written all over your murderous face." Kit chuckled. "You should do something about that if you feel that strongly."

"I plan to do just that. That is what brings me here. I would like you to take me to White's this evening after I see Frances home."

"You thinking of becoming a member?" The very notion seemed to shock his friend.

"No, of course not. I seek an audience with Lord Langford. I understand that he spends his evenings there and I think it's time I speak to him about marrying his daughter." Albert could not bear to take time away from Frances during his visits for an audience with her father.

"What? Now? Tonight? It can't wait until tomorrow?"

"You've already commented on my murderous aspect." Albert wasn't about to allow any more time pass than needed. "I think I've waited long enough, don't you?"

Kit must have realized there was no getting around it. Albert would insist, would keep insisting.

"I expect you are right."

"Lady Langford, Frances, and I will depart within the hour. I shall return for you and we can continue on to St. James' Street."

"I shall write to his lordship and alert him that he should expect visitors." Kit motioned for a footman and relayed his need to pen a missive. "The topic of matrimony isn't the type of thing one drops into another's lap without some type of warning."

Eleven

"How do you do, Lady Emmeline?" Mr. Hugh Gilbert, who looked from all outward appearances, quite ordinary, did not seem to display any of the *oddness* Lady Frances had indicated. His speaking voice was pleasant. He stood erect, holding his head held high in a manner she would not have expected from a simple *Mister*.

"How do you do, Mr. Gilbert?" Emmeline smiled and observed her new acquaintance with careful consideration.

His straight, brown hair, expressive eyes, and slightly rounded shoulders announced him as an amiable gentleman. Although she had to admit that sensitivity to grass and horses would be limited while in a ballroom which made it impossible to lament about his afflictions.

"I have heard much about you...about your *beauty*," said Mr. Gilbert upon their acquaintance. "I cannot say what I've heard is an exaggeration."

"If that was meant as a compliment, I shall gladly have it, sir. Thank you." Em found his appeal as a suitor quite good. Not for herself but for a certain young lady...if only they could find

93

something in common...an interest or an opinion. Emmeline had the most splendid scheme in mind.

"Ah...there you are, Lady Amelia." Em was most eager to greet the young lady Amelia had brought with her. "Miss Danvers, how nice it is to see you this evening."

"Lady Emmeline," Miss Danvers greeted her with a slight incline of her head. She and Em had exchanged Calls over the course of the last several weeks.

It began with the serious discussion over Lord Hoswell's attentions, and subsequently Em had issued the cut direct once she'd discovered his treachery. She thought Teresa Danvers kind and undeserving of such an unfeeling brute and deserved to find someone who understood her.

"I beg your pardon...." Em stepped back to reveal Frances and Mr. Gilbert standing to her right. "Of course you recall Lady Frances, she has just now returned from being absent from Society for far too long. I have just made the acquaintance of Mr. Gilbert." Em motioned to the gentleman then back to the ladies. "Mr. Gilbert, may I present Lady Amelia and Miss Danvers."

After the requisite exchanges of *How do you dos*, the group fell into a little silence. Both seemed equally as shy, Miss Danvers and Mr. Gilbert were more than willing to allow the others around them to carry the conversation. Em needed to set them at ease and coax them into speaking to one another. But how to do such a thing with so many people about?

Emmeline drew a flower adorning her hair and held it. Perhaps a bit too close to Miss Danvers who promptly sneezed. Twice.

This drew Mr. Gilbert's immediate attention. Without any further persuading from Em, and to her delight, he had much to say on the subject to Miss Danvers who listened and replied with equal insight and trepidation.

LORD LANGFORD SAT IN HIS FAVORITE CHAIR, IN HIS FAVORITE ROOM of his favorite club, White's. A glass of brandy in one hand and a cigar in his other. His companion, Lord Kennington, kept him company in the adjacent chair, his hand occupied with much the same drink and smoking vices. They did not speak much, both men merely enjoyed the camaraderie of the other or only when a thought happened to occur to either one of them.

"Great luck we have tonight, eh, Langford? On our own tonight, we can do as we like, no parties to attend...."

"Or host."

"Argh! Ain't that the worst?" Kennington puffed on his cigar. "I admit there is no escaping that fate for any of us."

"You've the right of it, Kennington. We each must do the pretty when it's our turn comes around."

"Wives wouldn't have it any other way."

"Probably wouldn't do it if it were not for the wives!" Langford's slight cough as he inhaled turned into a mighty chortle.

"It could be Raley or Barrington here instead of me in this chair." He pointed to its arm with his cigar. "In two days' time it might be."

"It may very well be." Langford sat up in his chair. "Barrington is having a *do* this evening as we speak. That's where my lady's gone, went to see Lady Barrington with Frances in tow. It's the first time she's gone out since...since...." He couldn't bring himself to mention that horrid abduction. "Just a bit concerned, you know."

"Of course, you are her father." Kennington leaned back to cross his legs in front of him. "You know what we need, Langford?"

"What's that?"

"A good, strong family connection." Kennington nodded, approving of his own idea. "Your family and mine."

"What's that you say?" Langford squinted in disbelief and regarded the man next to him. "I only have three girls."

"Ah, I see.... I do have Epping...*Nicholas,* only just eighteen. He may be a bit young for your Frances but what about your middle girl?"

"Eugenia?" Langford remained impassive. "That one is quite headstrong. No one is going to tell *her* who she can marry."

"Ah...a bit like my Emmeline, I see." Kennington's brows rose. "Well, that matchmaking business is better left to the ladies, anyway, don't you think?"

"For the most part, yes. Best we gentlemen keep out of it all together." Langford brought his glass to his lips.

A footman quietly entered and lowered a salver to Langford's side.

"For me, is it?" He set his glass on the small table next to him before taking the missive. He recognized the hand who had addressed it, Sir Christopher Glory's, and broke the seal. Langford cleared his throat to gain Kennington's attention before speaking. "Mr. Winslow seeks to meet with me this evening and begs that I remain until his arrival."

"Is he a member?" Kennington probably had no knowledge of the man.

"No. He's here from Somerset, just visiting for the Season." As Langford understood from Winslow himself, he had not been in Town for many years and his acquaintances were few.

"Ah. I see." Kennington puffed on his cigar. "I've had two of those sorts of *meetings* just the other day." He indicated the letter with the nod of his head.

"*Those* sorts of meetings?" Langford echoed.

"If you read between the lines I'm sure you'll see the matrimonial aspect to it. It's a good thing we don't try to match her with Epping. Your Frances about to be spoken for."

Finally. It was about time Winslow made his move.

THIS EVENING HELD MANY *FIRSTS* FOR EMMELINE. HER COMPANY AT the Barrington party was thin and if she wished for company, it would be up to her.

After arriving, more than an hour ago, Em approached Sir Garrett Hudson. Standing to one side of the room, his wounded arm in a sling and turned to the wall, keeping it out of the way. Because of his limited ability to avoid her, Em chose to approach him first.

As with the introduction of Miss Danvers and Mr. Gilbert, Em employed the help of Lady Amelia, leaving Frances to a somewhat anxious and very protective Mr. Winslow. Something about Mr. Gilbert's presence, which had been very limited as far as time spent with Frances, did not sit well with her young man.

Amelia, who had first inquired if Sir Garrett would speak to Emmeline, relayed his answer and returned to the small group of friends who had begun to gather around Em. He said he would be agreeable, allowing her to speak to him. Emmeline then asked Amelia if she could find Miss Lucy Carter and intervene after some twenty or thirty minutes.

Em asked Amelia for a favor which she did without question and would explain when they had a free moment.

After Emmeline and Sir Garrett greeted one another, she requested they should find somewhere comfortable and sit while conversing, which he agreed to without hesitation. He settled onto the chair and appeared to be in good spirits when they began.

He, without exception, accepted her apology and believed it not to be necessary. Sir Garrett freely admitted that Em's refusal to his marriage proposal was completely expected. At the moment he had held an unrealistic hope that since she had refused Lord Robert that she had preferred him. Now he understood that it was a futile attempt since he was the loser of the duel.

With the exception of his arm, it did not appear to Em that he was seriously injured. The blood loss he sustained was little but the shedding of blood cost him the duel.

It was no matter that his wound was not life-threatening or sizable, an injury was still an injury. As sorry as Emmeline was about his arm, there was no one who could wring the sympathy washing-cloth more efficiently than—

"*Miss Carter*! Lady Amelia! How kind of you to join us." The two swept toward Emmeline as if they arrived on a breeze. She stood at once and Sir Garrett followed suit. "I beg your pardon, sir." Emmeline swept her arm toward the newcomers. "Do you happen to be acquainted with Lady Amelia and Miss Carter?"

Sir Garrett gazed from one lady's face to the other, his smile widened. "I'm afraid I haven't had the pleasure."

The ever kind-hearted Miss Carter, who had noticed the gentleman's bandaged arm set in a sling anchored around his neck, returned his gaze with one of her own...silent, with a touch of concern, and thoroughly filled with compassion.

Em made the introductions and after all was said and done, Miss Carter began asking Sir Garrett questions. The gentleman, showing interest in the young lady, made more inquiries. Soon, Em and Amelia were left out of their conversation completely. They stepped back and quietly fading from the couple. Where, Emmeline declared, they would not be missed.

"Shouldn't Miss Carter's chaperone attend her?" Amelia glanced about, then gave up when it was apparent no chaperone existed.

"If she had a proper chaperone, that woman would *know* the location of her charge," Em replied. "You can stay if you'd like."

"Emmeline, where are you off to?"

"I must seek out Lord Robert. I'm afraid offering him an apology will be far more difficult. *If* he will allow me to approach." She moved away, leaving Amelia to stand off to the side as an observer and perhaps lend some needed propriety to the mutual admiration of Miss Carter and Sir Garrett.

On the far side of the second reception room stood Lord Robert Blair. Em really needed to pluck up her courage if she were to speak to him. One deep breath was hardly adequate. Two or three did not seem to improve her spirits. She closed her eyes for a few moments and convinced herself she must act now and would no longer allow herself to put off the deed. Opening her eyes and exhaling, she approached him, not knowing if it was the bravest or most foolish thing she ever had to do.

She needed to apologize, profusely, for her indolent refusal to his offer of marriage. She had done him a great disservice and he would be well within his right if he did not speak or acknowledge her.

Whether she liked it or not, she had to make the attempt. Em truly had owed him that much. It would be up to him if he chose to forgive her.

Em knew she possessed the courage it took to confront Lord Robert. If she could withstand an altercation with Martin Chandler, with his hateful words and harsh accusation, she certainly could approach Lord Robert who would never address her in near the venom *that* man had. The qualities of Lord Robert Blair were so superior that of...of.... So why had Emmeline refused him?

It was nothing more than that she did not care for him. He was a handsome, good-natured, and very brave man to have dueled for her but...she did not *love* him. Which brought her back to what Martin had said and she profoundly loathed thinking back to their conversation in the conservatory. She didn't want to think of him now. Not *that* man or *his* horrid, hurtful words.

"Lord Robert? Is it possible for me to have a word with you?"

He did her the honor of acknowledging her with an imperious nod of his head. Em was actually grateful for that. Lord Robert looked very different from the last time she'd seen him. His face was drawn and he did not smile. There appeared to be an attempt as the corner of his mouth twitched.

She offered him a gentle smile and did her utmost to hold his attention. He appeared more uncomfortable than she, if that was possible. No longer did she see traces of a spell she had once cast over him. He had been cured, rendered immune, and it was apparent the man who remained appeared very forlorn and sad.

Lord Robert was gracious enough to allow Em to say her peace. It seemed that her heart-felt words had no effect on him. She had meant them. The sincere apology, given freely, expressing her extreme regret. The misdirection she may have inadvertently, or not, intended. She tried to relay her great sorrow for any pain she caused him from the very bottom of her heart.

Had she done this? From what she could see she had stripped him of happiness and offended every good feeling. She could not bear it that she'd placed another person in such distress.

*I thought you better than that...*were Martin's words. Dwelling on them could cause her to cry, right here, right now, amongst these people.

With her regrets and apology concluded, Lord Robert bowed, excused himself, and walked away. Emmeline watched his retreating back and deemed her actions were not near enough. After regarding Lord Robert's tolerant expression, she felt she needed to do more but could not imagine what the *more* would be.

twelve

A VERY LARGE BOUQUET of peonies, hydrangeas, and forget-me-nots graced the foyer table when Frances stepped onto the main floor the next morning. They were beautiful.

"These have come for you." Lady Langford made a quiet but great fuss over the flowers, searching through the foliage.

"Who are they from, I wonder? There is no good reason for me to receive these. I did not dance at the Barrington's house party last night." Discounting Lord Adolphus' offering, the ones he thought might make up for his unacceptable behavior, It had been *a very long time* since Frances had been sent flowers.

"One does not receive a tribute from a gentleman unless—" Her ladyship was currently making a search between the stems looking for a card or note. "Ah!" She withdrew a calling card and stared at the name. "Not even *this* gentleman?"

Frances saw, clearly printed on the card: *Mr. Albert Winslow.*

The knocker sounded and Joseph opened the front door to reveal the very man. Albert stepped inside, appearing composed and quite dapper but not any different than he had previously.

"Good morning!" Albert greeted them just as he handed the butler his hat.

The two ladies stared at him, instantly becoming silent.

Albert stilled and the smile from his lips faded before glancing behind him, around him, looking a bit confused as though he had just come in the middle of something. "I beg your pardon, ladies. Am I disturbing you? It seems that you are in the middle of—"

"No, sir," Frances replied. "We have just now realized you sent these."

Albert glanced from Frances to the bouquet and his smile returned. "Yes, I did. I am glad they've arrived." He studied the floral arrangement and proclaimed, "They are quite splendid!"

"Yes, they are glorious...but I am at a loss, sir." Albert had not sent flowers before. For Frances, flowers from a gentleman always carried some sort of expectation, implying more than platonic interest. It was true they used one another's Christian names but that did not indicate any serious, personal attachment. They did more so out of convenience.

Only recently had she begun to think along *those* lines...the *wouldn't-it-be-nice* scenarios drifted through her head when she shared his company. He had always been agreeable but had never shown her outright affection and she was content with the self-imposed boundaries they shared. She expected their feelings would never progress, he had said as much to her weeks ago...he had not come to Town *in search of a wife.*

Frances felt very comfortable in his company. He had been a good friend to her.

But with the arrival of the flowers....

"They are to show my appreciation and...*admiration* for you, my lady," Albert replied.

"Really?" Frances smiled and unashamedly glanced up to

meet his eyes. She dared not hope that his intent was near what she'd wished. Could it be true? Could Albert have the same feelings for her she had for him?

Lady Langford cleared her throat, very delicately, as Lord Langford entered the foyer.

"I thought I heard voices out here."

"Good morning, your lordship." Albert greeted Frances' father with an incline of his head.

"*Winslow,*" Lord Langford reciprocated. "Good day to you. Here for your morning walk with Frances?"

"Yes, sir." Something about Albert seemed *off* to Frances. His behavior was a bit stiff, awkward. The tone of his voice was unnaturally elevated.

She looked from him to her father. Something was going on between them, or had she imagined it?

"Do keep a look-out for the wee-nest in the ivy of the oak on the west side. I think it's a pair of blue tits, been watching them come and go for some time now. Do let me know if they've finally settled on some eggs."

What? Had Frances' father gone mad? Why was he going on about wild birds?

"Yes, sir. I certainly shall." Albert replied enthusiastically and offered her his arm. "Lady Frances...shall we be off?"

Frances moved to Albert's side and placed her hand in the crook of his arm, as she often had. Why had this day felt so different than any other?

"Good." Lord Langford winked. *Winked...*he actually *winked* at Albert.

"My lord?" Lady Langford's questioning tone told Frances her mother was equally as confused as she by his lordship's behavior.

"Come along, my lady." Lord Langford offered his wife his

arm and placed her hand upon his arm. "I have something of importance to discuss with you...in my library."

Lady Langford's parting glance to Frances, as they were led in opposite directions, reaffirmed the notion that she was not the only person wondering if something odd was going on.

MARTIN ACCOMPANIED PAULINE AND JANE STILES TO THE LENDING library this warm, bright morning. Kit had told Martin it was *his turn,* before leaving him free to make his Morning Calls. Kit had previously taken the girls shopping, at the cost of three bonnets...*three?* Martin did not quite understand how that came to be.

It had to be said that sharing the arduous task of accompanying one's little sister was certainly made less onerous when shared with her best friend...Jane. In addition Mrs. Heffelfinger, doing more preening than he remembered, as Jane's chaperone, was a welcome addition and shared the responsibility for both girls.

"I have not quite decided what I shall choose next." Pauline was very much of a mind that held a single purpose and, as such a person, she limited her reading to one story at a time. "I shall see what is on offer."

"I hope they have the next volume in my story, I would hate to have to wait for the following installment." Jane was considered to be the more adventurous and voracious reader of the two. "I suppose I could find something new."

Martin did not know if her influence was wholly a welcome one on Pauline. Jane fancied what might be called 'independent thinking' could not have been a good thing. It would certainly make a gentleman think twice before considering he wanted a wife with such a quality.

They'd arrived and a gentle tinkle of a bell sounded as the door opened, allowing the four to enter. Pauline and Jane entered the establishment still chatting about Lord-only-knows-what...followed by Mrs. Heffelfinger. Martin came to an abrupt stop once inside.

"Gracious...not *him*!" Martin abruptly, staring down at his feet as to hide his face, removed his hat to shield his face from certain recognition.

"Whatever is the matter, Mr. Chandler?" Mrs. Heffelfinger pulled him to one side, away from the door, sensing his distress.

"Stay with the girls," he whispered as loudly as he dared without being overheard. "I shall join you when I am able."

Mrs. Hefflefinger nodded and scurried to catch up with the young ladies.

When Pauline turned to look for the rest of her party saw no-one until Mrs. Heffelfinger arrived some minutes later. "Where is Martin?"

"Your brother...is momentarily detained," Mrs. Heffelfinger uttered, out of breath and in some distress.

"Oh, I suppose he has finally found something that interests him," Pauline said lightly. That was a complete falsehood. From what she understood, this place held no interest for her brother. That was why he never brought her here. It took Sir Christopher to convince him that she and Jane needed to find some amusements and their choices were limited but they did need a chaperone and an escort if they wished to venture out-of-doors.

"Yes, I believe *someone* in the shop has caught his attention." Mrs. Heffelfinger was quick to point out. "I do not know who it is."

"Really?" Pauline touched Jane on the shoulder. She had

been listening but at the same time ran her fingers along the spines, skimming the book titles. "Come on, Jane. Let's find my brother."

Jane immediately followed, untying the ribbons under her chin and removing her bonnet.

"Martin! Martin—" Pauline snapped when she caught sight of her brother creeping around, slowly coming up behind them but clearly more interested in the aisles on either side.

Martin shushed her and maintained his covert behavior, stepping lightly across the floor.

"What are you doing? What is wrong with you?" Pauline had never seen him behave in this ridiculous manner.

"There's someone one here I'd rather not be seen by." He crushed the brim of his beaver with his fingers, holding it tightly against the palm of one hand.

"Who?" Pauline looked around, she saw no one.

"It is...*Hugh Gilbert*." He gave a rather loud, unconscious groan. "Under no circumstances do I wish for him to see me because that would cause him to address me. Then...he may wish to converse. Oh, *Lud*...I would never be free of him...." Just the mention of a conversation caused Martin's expression to pinch in discomfort.

Which caused Pauline to desperately wish to make his immediate acquaintance.

"He's with someone." Martin maintained his vigilance. "It is a lady."

"Really?" Jane became instantly interested. She came up behind Martin, setting her hands on his shoulders and leaning against him, trying to see for herself. "Who is she?"

"Get off, you!" Martin straightened, which pushed Jane back. "I did not see her face...all I saw was her hat," he grumbled and did not seem really all that interested in her identity. "The blasted edge blocked her face. Not that it matters, I can only feel sorry for the poor creature...being *trapped* in such a place as this...with *him* for company." Then added, "Can't imagine anything worse."

Mrs. Heffelfinger, who had not been involved in their *quiet* conversation, had strolled to the end of the aisle the three of them occupied. She made a very good show of casually browsing the book titles when she stepped back to wave, gaining Pauline's attention.

"*Here*!" Pauline nudged Jane and they tiptoed down the aisle in Mrs. H's direction until they reached her. All four of them, remaining very still and very quiet, removed some books, lowering the stack, to observe the couple in what they must have thought was a private moment.

They, Martin...she and Jane...should not have been watching. It was *very* bad of all of them.

"These have been the happiest weeks of my life," the man, presumably Hugh Gilbert, said to the young lady with him. His voice was gentle and filled with everything that was agreeable reinforced the feeling that they should not be witness to this exchange. This declaration was not to be shared with others but Pauline was unable to pull her attention away.

"Who *is* she?" Jane's urgent whisper posed the question all of them wanted to know. "*She* does not...perhaps *cannot* speak.... She must be overcome."

"We can't very likely approach her and *inquire*," Pauline replied rather strongly, then wondered if it would be *very* rude of her to do so.

"No. I suppose not." Jane's left hand, that rested on Pauline's shoulder, now tightened and her tense fingers dug in. "I wish they would say more instead of *gazing* at one another. It's *so* boring!"

"Like a pair of moon-calves, they are." Mrs. Heffelfinger mumbled. Pauline surmised that Martin was not so interested in what the couple said as much as keeping out of Mr. Gilbert's line of sight.

"Will you allow the use of our Christian names?" He took up her hand, brought it to his lips, and gazed intensely at her.

Jane averted her eyes. Unable to resist, her gaze returned to the couple a few moments later.

"I do not know, Mr. Gilbert," the lady replied. "My mother and my chaperone would only be a few minutes at the milliners next door. What if they should see us? It is quite improper."

"Let them catch us!" Mr. Gilbert said ready to challenge the propriety of the modern world. "There is nothing improper with our conduct, Miss Danvers...*Teresa.*"

Teresa Danvers? Neither Pauline nor Jane knew of her and their interest in the couple began to lose its appeal. There was nothing more to learn, no mystery as to the identity of the two. There was the slight intrigue of why Martin should fervently wish not to be seen by said gentleman but since that had to do with her brother's idiosyncrasies, Pauline did not much care.

The bell on the front door of the shop sounded, announcing new patrons or...Mrs. Danvers the chaperone. Their voices carried throughout the shop, alerting Mr. Gilbert and Miss Danvers their precious time alone had come to an end. After a short discussion among the four, their group departed.

"That was exciting." Jane must have truly enjoyed the skulking about and the mystery of the identity of the couple.

"For all of five minutes." Pauline found watching her brother far more entertaining.

"I wonder why Martin was so afraid to be seen by Mr. Gilbert?" Jane had not missed Martin's absurd reaction.

"I doubt Mr. Gilbert would have noticed Martin, he was far

too preoccupied with Miss Danvers." Pauline drew out her name in a dramatic fashion—"*Ter-re-sa*."

"Oh, go on. Pauline." Jane laughed. "Shall we choose our books?"

"Yes, let's do. Let us return to the front of the shop—that's where they keep the newer volumes."

"Good idea." Jane retied the ribbon of her bonnet and looped it around her arm. "We're heading to the front, Auntie. What about Martin? Shall we tell him where we've gone?"

"No." Pauline snickered. "Who cares if he's left behind?"

"I HAD NO IDEA YOUR FATHER HAD SUCH AN INTEREST IN WILD birds." Albert led Frances down the path in the rear gardens of Langford House as he had the day before.

"Neither did I." Frances felt completely befuddled with her father's talk of blue tits and Albert's continuation of the topic. Was this a mutual interest they had only just discovered? She had no idea either of them had a fascination for birds.

"You cannot tell me you took no notice of the blue tits flitting about during our strolls."

"I can't say I had." She recalled no such thing—ever. Frances couldn't help but look about, between the trees as they strolled toward the bench they frequented. She had been certain his interest lay in the story of the book they read and hopeful that her company might have been part of the appeal, not the birds.

Frances had to admit, if only to herself, that she was becoming more than fond of Albert. Rather attached to him, really.

"Blue tits have a white face and a slash of black over each eye. Their most distinctive markings is the bright yellow chest and tuft of blue on the tops of their heads and at the edge of their wings."

"I had no idea you were so knowledgeable about birds." Of course Frances knew the distinguishing marks of a blue tit. They were rather common.

The couple had arrived at their bench and he saw her settled on one end while he took his customary seat on the other side.

"I am by no means an expert of any kind. George Montagu has a very nice *Alphabetical Synopsis of British Birds,* an Ornithological Dictionary."

Then it came to her notice that Albert carried a book.

"That wouldn't happen to be a copy of George Montagu's dictionary, would it?" Not that Frances was overly enthusiastic that it might have been...but that had been their current topic of discussion for some minutes now.

Albert held the book outward as if noticing it for the first time. "Oh, heaven's no!"

With his unexpected appearance this morning, Frances has neglected to bring with her the book they were currently reading.

"But this is for you." He handed her the book. "Do open it, will you?"

"Very well," she said, taking the volume from him and glanced at the spine. *Simple Story*...it was the first volume. "You know that I've already read this?"

"You may have read this before but I guarantee you'll find for these characters that there will be an entirely different story inside...with an unexpected ending."

Frances wasn't sure what to make of this. Why all the intrigue? After opening the cover she turned the first few pages until she reached a small folded paper tucked between the pages. She glanced at Albert and again, with a nod, he urged her to continue.

She picked up the paper and unfolded it to read his hand-written message:

> *Dearest, Frances,*
> *Will you marry me?*
> *Albert*

"Albert...." She looked at him...gazed upon his face, into his kind, brown eyes before noticing that he had pulled his gloves off and held them in his hands. The discoloration had greatly faded into tinges of greens and yellows. He laid his gloves in the open pages of the book and took her hands into his. They were warm and his touch gentle.

"I love you." He shrugged in that modest, slightly shy manner that had become very familiar to her, and to be honest, she found the gesture endearing. "There is not another I respect or admire more. It is my wish that you return with me to Somerset as my wife. I cannot imagine my life would be complete without you."

"Albert...that is so very sweet." The touch of his bare hand against her skin took her breath away. It was difficult to focus on what he was saying.

Could it be that everything she had hoped for...wished for... was coming true?

To find a suitable, coherent reply seemed impossible. She found it beyond her ability to put into words what she was feeling.

"I hope that is not a kind way of refusing my offer."

"No, it is not." Frances felt slightly overwhelmed. This was far from her first offer of marriage and she did not wish to lunge at him with an acceptance. But unlike the other two offers she had received, this one held much more for her. "Of course I accept." She smiled, then laughed out loud, unable to keep her joy contained. "I am most happy to marry you, Albert. You have become quite important to me. It's not that I rely upon you but.... Since our return, I cannot tell you how much I looked forward to seeing you, to our time together, and to think" —her mind had already leapt ahead to their life as man and wife— "I should always treasure being with you."

"I am so very glad to hear you say that." He released her hands and touched the side of her face as he leaned near to kiss her lips. When they parted he whispered, "I *adore* you."

Albert's smile was glorious and, no doubt, reflected her own.

Frances felt so very happy. At one time she thought this could never be. In recent years it seemed she could not avoid adversity, no matter what her actions. Now...with Albert, everything seemed to fall into place. There were no missteps, no lapses in judgment.

He sat close to her on the bench with his arm draped behind her. She felt the comforting warmth of his arm across her shoulders. He took up one of her hands in his once again.

"Shall we tell my parents?"

"Of course, his lordship already knows. I asked for his permission to address you last night."

"Last night?" She straightened, coming out of her haze. "But we were at the Barrington house party."

"After that. I went to White's to see him." He rubbed the back of her hand with his thumb, an action that distracted her.

"Oh...." Recollection of his unanticipated appearance at Albert's unexpected arrival that morning and that uncharacteristic *wink* of his came to her. All of the odd behaviors somehow it all finally made sense. Her father knew what was to happen.

"What was the meaning of all that talk of the blue tits? First, father, then you?"

"Oh...it was nothing of importance, just to muddy the waters a bit...put you off your guard."

"Oh, it did that all right." What were these men about? Why could they not say what they meant? "I much prefer that you dispense with the diversionary maneuvers and rely on your persuasive techniques."

"And what would that be, dearest?" He stared at her as if he had no idea what she was about.

"Your soothing baritone is quite enticing. The manner in which you touch me...hold my hand, I find most satisfying. You could try to coax me with your kisses...which, I might add, have hardly been adequate in number. May I point out that we have been engaged for at least five minutes now and you have only kissed me once."

"I can see I am clearly derelict in my duty," he admitted. Frances could respect a man who could freely accept his faults without fear of sanction.

"Yes, sir, I'm afraid you are."

Albert did as requested, leaning closer to Frances and kissed his wife-to-be once again.

thirteen

THE NEXT MORNING, EMMELINE, with Mrs. Peckover only a step or two behind, was nearly prepared to leave for Morning Calls. Just as they stepped onto the ground floor, the butler had pulled the door open, revealing Lady Amelia.

"Amelia? What are you doing here?" Em arranged the ribbons under her chin, securing her bonnet. "You know I was going out today."

"I know but I had hoped to catch you before you left." Amelia seemed anxious and fidgeted with her reticule when she neared and whispered, "I have some news for you."

Em glanced at Mrs. Peckover who understood that they would be delayed while the two young ladies had their discussion.

"Do wait, Mrs. Bouvier," Amelia said to her chaperone once inside. "I shan't be long. I only need a moment or two of Lady Emmeline's time."

"Would you like to step into the front parlor?" Em motioned with the gloves she held tight in her left hand. Amelia strode past Em into the parlor and the doors were closed behind them.

"I have just come from calling on Miss Carter."

Lucy? What news of her did Amelia think imperative?

"You introduced her to Sir Garrett Hudson last night."

"Yes, I remember." Emmeline thought pairing the two was inspired and they very well may suit.

"I believe it is acceptable to tell you, since you were the one who introduced them, in the strictest of confidence, of course." A flush crept up Amelia's neck and washed onto her cheeks.

"Of course," Em agreed. If this was, indeed, news that needed to be kept to oneself, she would.

"They are *secretly* engaged," Amelia disclosed with delicious, muted excitement.

"What? After spending an evening together?" Instead of a tempting bit of *on-dit* Em thought it distressing. Even a perfectly matched couple must take some time to develop those long lasting feelings. It simply did not happen overnight. Infatuation, of course, but not the emotions needed to sustain a marriage.

"He is absolutely besotted with her, and she, with him." The jubilant news fairly flowed from Amelia's lips.

Em ran her finger between the ribbon that held on her bonnet and her neck, wondering if she had tied it too snug.

"Lucy tells me they could scarcely be parted last night. She was making preparations to visit him as I left."

"*She* planned to Call on *him*?" That *was* outrageous. Young ladies did *not* call on gentlemen.

"He has been wounded and only just out of his sick bed." The excuse Amelia offered was weak and completely unacceptable.

"He is well enough to attend a house party," Emmeline groused.

"But he did not dance," Amelia maintained. As if it were some sort of ultimate measure of fitness.

"Dancing is not the only method of mischief." This seemed very harum-scarum to Em. Miss Carter's behavior was impetuous. She should take more care, did she not understand that her reputation was at stake? "Their parents cannot approve of this type of slap-dash meeting."

"That is why their engagement is to be kept secret. Her parents are not opposed to Sir Garrett, *per se*. It is only the length of the acquaintance that concerns them," Amelia explained. "Lucy tells me they would not even contemplate a discussion of any marriage settlements until a fortnight has passed."

"That does not seem an excessive amount of time...two weeks is not all that long to wait." Em did not wish to side against the couple but what was asked of them was not unreasonable.

True love mattered but if one were to consider the circumstance of the rest of one's life one would wish to make certain they were making the correct choice.

Once done marriage was not easily undone.

"Yes, well...Lucy is very impatient and the days ahead are so many...long and difficult to bear when they are parted." The dramatics in which Amelia offered this sentiment did not strike the right note with Emmeline.

"*If*...they managed to remain together."

"How could you doubt their devotion? Are you not the one who brought them together? Do you not wish them happy?"

Love was certainly wonderful, especially new love. But it was not always earnest or enduring.

"You must wonder, Amelia...because Miss Carter does not seem to realize the circumstances in which her new beau sustained his injury?"

"Well, yes. Dueling *might* be understood as *scandalous*." The very notion of a person being tainted by scandal itself did not seem to affect Amelia.

"It is not exactly the duel to which I refer. Sir Garrett incurred his injury over his love of another lady, one to which he had offered marriage, only two days past." Emmeline pointed out. Yes, Amelia had known once because Em had told her, but apparently she had forgotten those unpleasant details.

"Perhaps you are right." Amelia's enthusiasm for the couple to dash off to marry became muted. "The prudent thing to do is for them to wait...just for a bit." Her disappointment in Em had evolved into some sensible reflection.

"I do believe a match between them is possible but one cannot rush headlong into these things. It may have been a mistake on my part to make them known to one another." But Em did not think so. "It simply occurred to me they may suit. I never expected they would act in such haste. Their futures are for them, and their parents, to decide."

"I suppose there is nothing for it and we shall have to wait to see how things work out." Amelia shook her head, clearly dissatisfied that she need wait.

"I am on my way to see Lady Frances Abbott." Emmeline turned her attention to drawing on her gloves, starting with the left. "She, too, is recuperating, and has a certain young man in her life. They've been acquainted for sometime now..." Em did not wish to say but she had her thoughts on the matter and smiled. "I expect she will be feeling more the thing soon."

SIR CHRISTOPHER GLORY WAVED HIS WALKING STICK IN THE direction of the group Martin led from across the road before making his way across to join them, which was not without some hazards.

"Fancy, meeting up with you all? What are the odds?" Kit made a fuss of brushing the wrinkles out of his garments... clearly to bring attention to his...*costume*.

"What *is* that you're wearing?" Martin squinted and turned his head to one side, trying to restrict the view of his friend's waistcoat.

"This?" Drawing the edges of his jacket slightly open, Kit allowed the group a view of what lay underneath.

"*Kit!* Must you do that here?" Jane complained, averting her gaze. "No one wishes to see *that!*"

Pauline uttered a forceful, "*Sir Christopher*, please!"

"You people simply have no taste, no sense of fashion acumen!" he grumbled. "I'll have you know this is *au courant,* one of Lorenzo's new masterpieces. It is reminiscent of daffodils or sunflowers with its vibrant yellow and slashes of green representing stems or leaves on a background of azure blue."

Martin dare not look. He had no idea if anyone else in their party would view the garment a second time or if they deemed a single exposure adequate.

"Is that what it is?" Pauline could not have sounded less interested and Jane snickered.

Little sisters, no matter whose, had the profound talent for knowing what to say and how to irritate an elder brother. In this case, it was Martin's sister goading Kit.

"I shall change the topic lest I say something I sincerely regret." Kit's jaw clenched in the attempt to staunch a retort, and perhaps restrain his temper.

"To prevent you from sounding like—"

"*Paul-line*," Martin intervened, sounding parental and imperious. "That is quite enough. On behalf of our mother, I ask that you mind your manners."

"Of course, brother." She turned her head and offered the baronet a smile. "I beg your pardon, Sir Christopher."

"Apology accepted, Miss Chandler." Kit went so far as to touch the brim of his hat.

There were a few moments of silence, allowing the atmosphere to cool.

"Dare I ask what causes our paths to cross? I thought you were occupied this morning." Relieved when Kit fell into step next to him, Martin need not openly avoid the waistcoat.

"My visit had been unexpectedly cut short."

"I wonder why?" Martin mumbled.

"What's that you say?"

"Nothing. Nothing at all." It was ridiculous to think anyone would alter their behavior due to a garment, no matter how unpleasant it appeared. But still…Martin could not like it. He found it quite distasteful, that would never change.

"It may interest you to know that my association with Miss Forbes has come to an end."

"And you wonder why she handed you the mitten…." Martin could not help but think his friend had not even a clue. "Even though I have not yet had the pleasure of making her acquaintance, I like her already. She shows discerning qualities and extremely good judgment. As well as a strong sense of self-preservation."

"It has nothing to do with my choice in attire, I can assure you. I believe she feels as I do…we simply do not suit. We parted on good terms. She has also requested that I make you known to her and I think you two may make an agreeable match."

"Me?" That did surprise Martin. To prefer his company over

Kit's elevated her in his esteem. He smiled. "I look forward to our acquaintance."

"Perhaps this evening at the Raley-do. You are planning to attend, are you not?"

"With the acquaintance of Miss Forbes awaiting me, how could I not?"

"Well put." Kit swung his walking stick forward. "Did you visit the lending library?"

"We did."

"I know it is not your favorite but...I'm certain our sisters enjoyed having a look around. Jane is forever wishing to go."

"I cannot think why," Martin groused. "I have never dreaded it so much in my life."

"It's not exactly my favorite but I far prefer the books in my own library. Why do you say that?"

Pauline paused and turned to explain. "Martin saw someone he did not wish to see."

"Oh?" Kit looked interested, shifting his gaze from Pauline to Martin. "Who would that be?"

"Mr. Gilbert, I expect," Jane filled in.

"How did you two know his name?" Martin was fairly certain there were no introductions performed, at least none that he saw.

"He is not known to us but you told us yourself, do you not recall?" Pauline replied. "And we heard Miss Danvers' refer to him as such."

"How did you discover the identity of the young lady?" Martin was aghast.

"From Mr. Gilbert...Miss Danvers..." Jane replied then imitated dramatically, "*Ter-re-sa!*"

"You were eavesdropping! We are derelict in guiding our

younger sisters through the shoals of social decorum, Kit, what would our mothers say?"

"It is hardly our role to teach etiquette. What makes this worse is that their behavior may have an adverse affect on our reputations. Who knew they were such nosy-busybodies?" Kit was able to retaliate from his earlier encounter with Pauline and now had his chance to have his revenge. "No better than Town *gossips!*"

"We cannot ignore what goes on right under our noses!" Jane proclaimed.

"I have no ongoing guidance from an elderly relative to proper conduct...." Pauline confessed, sounding forlorn.

"Well, thank you very much." Mrs. Heffelfinger responded, clearly insulted. Pauline had belittled her influence, as minor as it was, as well.

"Especially when it comes to fending off cads!"

"*Cads?*" Kit recoiled in what Martin found, a comedic manner. He did not quite understand why the two continued to have at each other. It was rather pointless, very juvenile, truth be told. "Did you hear that, Martin? Your sister thinks *I* am a cad."

"I pray *you* do not take offense, Mrs. H." Martin disregarded Kit's complaint. "You are not *my* aunt."

"Might as well be...." she murmured. "As much time as I see to your *social decorum*—the two of you are joined at the hip."

"Which brings me to something I would like to discuss with you, Martin." Kit paused and motioned for Mrs. Heffelfinger to continue forward. The females bent their heads together in laughter before marching ahead.

"I am finding it such a trial to keep Jane *occupied*, and there are many weeks left. I expect you are finding the same issue with Pauline."

"I am glad she is not Out yet, Kit, but...in some ways that

would be preferable, she would have more friends, more parties, and not be so reliant on me...*us* to entertain her—them. Having you and Jane sharing the same situation does help. They do keep one another company, thank heavens."

"Is your mother set on bringing Pauline Out next year?"

"It is not something she discusses with me...but as I understood that was the plan." Martin wasn't certain he could tolerate another Season because his mother would insist he return with them.

"I was thinking that may work for Jane as well. It would be good for the two to be with one another."

"Must we speak of this now...it is so very depressing."

"Agreed." A minute or two passed and Kit spoke again. "Where are we headed?"

"To call on Lady Frances Abbott. I have made her acquaintance but do not know much about her...with the exception of her involvement in *the incident*."

"You know enough." Kit's serious glance from under the brim of his beaver was enough to quell any questions Martin may have had on the topic. "Suffice it to say she's a *cousin* of ours."

"Why am I not surprised?" Martin quipped. Honestly, the only family Kit was not related to was his own.

"I have had a suggestion on how to occupy their time. But I must be honest, I'm not certain I can endorse it."

"Is it yours?" Martin arched an eyebrow.

"Partially...Jane's really."

"I think this may be problematic." Martin wasn't certain he wanted to hear a recommendation from someone who had more than their own agenda in mind. Was that not the issue they faced previously? Young ladies who did not understand how to navigate London Society?

"This concerns" —Kit leaned closer to whisper— "*Monsieur Philippe.*"

"Oh, that fellow." Martin knew of him from his appearance at a recent gathering. It did not take a mind-reader to discern Jane's feelings regarding the dancing master. The younger members of Society seemed to be rather taken with the foreigner. Whether she fancied him or it was a mere infatuation Martin could not say but he completely understood his friend's hesitancy in selecting the *Monsieur* to instruct their young ladies. "Something's dodgy, there."

"Jane retrieved his card while at Lady Chesney's party and presented it to me in hopes that I would retain his services."

"Lady Kennington engaged him for an evening...a private lesson for the *younger* members of their party. I cannot say I have a specific complaint regarding him but...." Martin thought something about the man unsettling.

"Exactly. Dancing lessons would keep the girls occupied. As Jane put it...this must be addressed next year if they are to return." Kit waved his hand as if pushing aside the notion. "I told her I would *consider* it, and I am nowhere near making up my mind. Although, if you feel strongly either way, I would take your opinion into consideration."

Martin drew in a breath comprehending Kit's dilemma. The decision was not Martin's to make and needed to be left up to his mother.

"Unless I am mistaken, *you* will need to return next year in any case, am I right?" Martin felt one side of his mouth lift. It was his opinion that Kit was stepping closer to the petticoat line...only inching, perhaps, but moving, never-the-less, closer.

"*What-cha* mean?" Kit replied.

"It cannot have escaped my notice that you have been quite

the man about town lately...courting more ladies than I can ever recall."

"I am here now...I don't see why I shouldn't give it a go." Pushing his brim away from his face, Kit regarded Martin in a dubious manner. "Neither one of us is immune, you know."

"You may not be, but I think I have had enough this Season, no offense to Miss Forbes." Martin was confident in his path. "Been soured on the whole love and marriage bit. I realize I had been headed in that direction but I got it all wrong. I dare say I am not a good candidate."

"And I was beginning to think you were merely unlovable," Kit teased. "Apparently you are impossible as well."

"That may well be for the present. Perhaps not forever." Martin was past feeling sorry for himself, merely accepting his life as it was. "Tell me about Miss Forbes...."

"Ahh...." Kit crooned, pointing his index finger at him. "So you *are* interested in her."

"I wouldn't say *interested*...more *curious*, perhaps." Martin did not have matrimony in mind, however, he was never one to say *nay* to the opposite sex.

"Miss Forbes is all that is kind. She is compassionate, quiet, if that is your preference in ladies."

"And you don't?" Martin thought Kit wished for a quiet-type of companion.

"I thought it was. I found her...a bit...dull? I mean that in the nicest possible way."

"Of course. How else would one accept being called *dull*?" Then it occurred to him.... "You did not say that *to* her, did you?"

"Oh, no! I would never be so indelicate." Kit was as much a gentleman as Martin believed.

"And did you say what her given name was?"

"Miss Forbes'?" Kit turned to his friend and intoned, in the kindest tone. "Nancy."

"Nancy...." Martin repeated softly, deciding if he liked it. "*Nancy*," he said again. Yes, he mused and smiled. He liked it well enough.

"Ahh.... Here we are! " Kit swung his walking stick out in front of them and pointed. Pauline and Jane began to hurry as they approached. "Langford House."

fourteen

EMMELINE HAD THOUGHT TO stop in at Langford House this morning. She was not yet in the mood to face others and craved a more sedate visit. Calling on Lady Frances would be the perfect way to begin.

"Lady Emmeline—what an utter surprise! I am so delighted to see you." Frances swept into the entrance hall from the front parlor to greet her. Em was taken aback at how well her friend appeared. Perhaps getting out of the house and back into Society did her good. "You must come into the parlor and sit and I shall call for tea."

The butler pulled the front door open again, very wide this time, allowing a number of people to enter. A pair of young ladies stepped inside.

"Look who is here, Pauline!" Jane, with a widening smile, held her right hand out to Em.

"Lady Emmeline!" Pauline, who seemed equally as pleased, rushed to Em's side to greet her.

"And Cousin Frances!" Jane dipped a curtsy and clasped her cousin's hand with her left.

"So very many visitors all at once!" Frances appeared quite delighted at the sight of the four friends together again but looked around the newcomers to see the gathering in the entry hall. "Who have you brought with you?"

"With the exception of Mrs. Heffelfinger and our brothers, there are no others," Jane replied.

"Honestly, I think that is quite enough," Mrs. Heffelfinger remarked and stepped aside, keeping out of the way.

"*Brothers*?" Em was completely delighted with the arrival of Jane and Pauline, she hadn't noticed the others. There was something rather bothersome with the intrusion of gentlemen on an all-ladies visit. Turning to do the pretty, Em presented a smile and curtsied. "Sir Christopher, good morning."

"And to you, Lady Emmeline." He touched the brim of his hat, not yet having removed it. "How nice it is to see you again."

Then she caught sight of the other *brother*...Miss Chandler's, and how Em could have forgotten that *he* was related to such an amiable, likable young lady, Emmeline would never know.

"*Mr. Chandler.*" Emmeline could almost feel her blood turn cold within her veins as she uttered his name. The smile on Em's face became immobile and the words that came to her, all rude, fought for exposition. She could neither alter nor remove her facial expression, and she said nothing more.

"Lady Emmeline," were his curt words. This was not accompanied by any other civility.

The man was hateful. The memory of their last encounter flared into her mind. How dare he speak to her in that manner. How *dare* he.... She would show him. Em had every intention of proving Martin Chandler wrong. She was not the horrid creature he proclaimed her to be.

"I certainly hope we have enough lemon cake for everyone,"

Lady Langford remarked and sent one of the footmen to the kitchen for an answer.

The countess need not worry, for Em heard Mr. Chandler say to Sir Christopher after a gentle nudge, "I think there are more than enough visitors, Kit. If you don't mind taking charge of our party, I shall be off."

Sir Christopher's gaze shifted from his friend to Emmeline and back again. His expression said it all, clearly understanding the miasma between the two well-enough and accepted with a nod of his head.

As she once thought him *dull*, the baronet had seemed insightful to relieve the tension, for Em at least, by allowing Mr. Chandler to depart.

"I bid you farewell and good luck. Do give them all my apologies for leaving so soon." Mr. Chandler glanced about, successfully avoiding eye contact with Emmeline, and slipped from the residence without notice.

"Frances...." Lady Langford had to navigate the room to touch her daughter's shoulder to gain her attention. "Why do you not take your friends inside. I'll send in a tray."

"Thank you, Mama." Frances attempted to herd the trio of young ladies to the double doors.

"Why, yes, Sir Christopher," Mrs. Heffelfinger said in a rather loud voice. "I would love to take a turn in the rear gardens." She waited for him to offer his arm, holding her hand in the air.

The attentive baronet offered his escort, placing his forearm under her hand. "If you ladies will excuse us." Sir Christopher nodded before departing with Mrs. Heffelfinger for their stroll.

Frances led the way into the front parlor followed by the continual chatter of Pauline and Jane with Em trailing. Her attention was not on the couple leaving toward the back of the house but the lone gentleman whom, she felt, had abandoned their party.

It was Mr. Chandler's duty to attend to his sister and not task another with her care. How rude and unkind of him to leave her.

"Are you bothered that the gentlemen have left us?" Frances asked Em when she finally caught up with the other three. Pauline and Miss Stiles had fallen quiet, all gazing at Emmeline.

"The gentlemen?" Em quipped in a nonchalant tone. "I could not give a fig that they've not joined us."

"Oh, I think it's better to be left alone with one another, don't you agree, Pauline?" Jane uttered on a sigh. "I much prefer keeping our own company, just us ladies."

"*Your* brother may be more considerate, domesticated than mine. Martin can be abominable." Pauline turned from the two seated with her to address the only one who still stood, lingering at the open door. "Isn't that so, Emmeline?"

"What's that you say, Pauline?" Emmeline replied, turning in their direction. She appeared somewhat distracted to Frances.

"She and Martin do not rub along well," Pauline whispered to the two sitting with her.

"Really?" Frances understood the two families were close and the news about Emmeline and Mr. Chandler's antagonistic interaction came across as a bit shocking.

"You should see how he goes on about her...not in a *kind* manner, I would say." Pauline glanced at Emmeline. "I beg your pardon, Lady Emmeline. I do not mean to sound—"

"Not to worry, Pauline. You are not saying anything of which I am not already aware." Emmeline's chin lifted, she did so clearly in defiance.

Frances thought there wasn't a man who could resist Emmeline's charm, well...not *all men*. The thought of her Albert made her smile. "Goodness, I had no idea Mr. Chandler felt so strongly about you."

"*Strongly?* I cannot believe anyone would wish for *strong* feelings?" Emmeline turned away, toward the table that held her beautiful flowers. "He does not even show me the least bit of civility. He has been—he has *said* some very unkind things to me."

"I think he's funny." Cousin Jane snickered.

"That is an odd thing to say." It occurred to Frances she did not know Mr. Chandler at all. One thought him unpleasant, the other funny? Pauline's opinion of her own brother could not be depended upon, her connection would certainly bias her judgement, good or ill.

How could she align these differing impressions of the same man?

"Just this morning he was hiding behind a stack of books at the lending library." Pauline laughed at her own brother.

"You shouldn't say it that way. It makes him sound like a coward." Jane joined in her friend's laughter. "He simply did not wish to be seen."

"Mr. Gilbert had no interest in Martin. He was completely engrossed with Miss Danvers. I don't think he noticed anyone."

"What's that you say?" It seemed that Lady Emmeline had lost all interest in the discussion of Mr. Chandler and his various behaviors and became intrigued with the couple mentioned. She glanced at Frances before asking, "Mr. Gilbert *and* Miss Danvers in the lending library?"

"You only just introduced them last night." Frances recalled how Lady Emmeline insisted upon meeting Mr. Gilbert. It was not that she was interested in him for herself, but now it was apparent, by the mischievous twinkle in her eyes and the slight smile it had brought to her lips, that she had every intention of matching him with Miss Danvers.

"Yes, they appeared quite...cozy together," Pauline confessed.

"We shouldn't have been listening." Jane grew quiet and seemed remorseful.

"It was difficult to ignore them, don't you think? It was quiet and Martin didn't wish to be seen."

Jane giggled.

"What did they say?" Emmeline was keen to learn if a romance was developing. Frances understood that was Emmeline's reason for introducing the two last night. She thought them a perfect match.

"It's not quite an *on-dit* anyone would want to know but...." Pauline hesitated then continued. "Mr. Gilbert said he was very happy to be in her company. Miss Danvers appeared to be quite affected."

"Gracious, all they did was stare at one another," Jane added with a sigh of exasperation.

"I think he may have pressed her hand." Had that been speculation or had that been seen?

"He may have," Jane confirmed.

"And Mr. Gilbert asked if Miss Danvers would permit use of their Christian names," Pauline continued.

"Miss Danvers said she was afraid her mother and her chaperone would discover them together." The pitch of Jane's voice rose when the threat of discovery became imminent.

"Mr. Gilbert did not care! He maintained that there was nothing improper with his feelings for her."

"And then" —Jane drew out— "He called her—*Teresa!*"

"My word!" Frances wasn't certain what shocked her more...

the seemingly shy Mr. Gilbert's daring at using Miss Danvers' Christian name or how swift they had progressed in their romance.

The news of the couple seemed to cheer Lady Emmeline. Her entire demeanor altered. She stood straighter and her confident air, that had deflated with the encounter with Mr. Chandler, had returned to that of a very self-assured young lady.

Emmeline moved across the room and approached the table with the flowers. "What an *exceptional* floral arrangement." For Emmeline to give such high praise to something that must have been so ordinary warmed Frances' heart. She knew her friend had received more than a dozen flowers over the course of the last month.

"They're from Albert."

"*Albee*?" Jane dared to say Mr. Winslow's name, the one Sir Christopher used. The one, Frances surmised, her cousin was not allowed to utter when in either of the gentlemen's company. It certainly was far too familiar and their association not close enough for it to be acceptable.

But Jane used the moniker all the same.

"Yes, that's right." Frances felt a smile stretch across her face. She could not prevent the excitement she felt inside from emerging. She pressed the palms of her hands to her warming cheeks. *Oh, dear*. Her secret...*their* secret would not remain so much longer.

"*Lady Frances*?" Jane and Pauline chorused.

"Is there something you wish to tell us?" Emmeline turned to regard Frances.

This was the moment. Why should Frances have felt nervous or embarrassed? Was it that her new fiancé was known to them all? She had never had such a group of friends who cared about the particulars of her life.

"Yes, well...." Frances didn't exactly know what to say then realized she should tell them...say the words out loud. "I've agreed to marry Albert Winslow."

"*Wot*?"

"You've been keeping this from us all this time? What wonderful news!"

The three cheered. They were absolutely beside themselves with joy. If it was possible, the well-wishes of her friends made this a more joyous occasion.

"How could you have not told us? When did this happen? How did he ask you? When will you be married? Will it be soon? How long have you been engaged?"

The questions came fast, Frances wasn't certain who asked what. This was all very confusing. She was excited and happy and was so very glad she was able to share her good news with these ladies. "It's only happened...just this morning."

"Where is he? Where is Albee? Why isn't he here with you now? Are we to expect him?"

"I do not know where he is at this precise moment." Frances felt a giggle inside struggling to emerge—so many questions from only two impulsive, inquisitive young ladies.

Displaying some knowledge of marriages and weddings, Emmeline's query was more mature in nature. "Will you be married by license? Perhaps by Special License?"

"Neither of us are in a great hurry," Frances replied. He had explained how he wanted them to take their time and do things properly...not in a slap-dash manner. "Albert would prefer to remain in Town and enjoy the rest of the Season. I can't say I blame him after all that has happened." She knew her friends understood. "We have agreed to marry by banns, after the final reading at the end of next month. Once we are wed we will remove to his estate in Somerset."

"You are to be wed here? Will we be allowed to attend? Will there be a party after? A wedding breakfast?" The non-stop questions continued from Jane and Pauline.

"My goodness! What is going on—ladies...*ladies*.... Please." Lady Langford entered, purposely interrupting the inquiries.

"I beg your pardon, Lady Langford." Jane, after falling immediately silent, was quick to offer an explanation for their boisterous behavior. "Cousin Frances was telling us her good news!"

"We are so very excited that she is to be married!" Pauline continued. "We were asking about her plans."

"I can well imagine *what* is being discussed but *really*.... I have no doubt you could do so in a more *temperate* manner."

"Yes, ma'am," both Jane and Pauline replied and appeared immediately repentant.

"Lord Langford and I are very pleased about Frances' match. Mr. Winslow is an admirable man and he is most welcome into our family, after an unprecedented, trying time." Her ladyship threw her arms wide and announced. "That is all behind us. Now we have a wedding, and their modest festivities, to plan."

"*Modest?* You certainly wish to make more of a celebration." Emmeline, who surely would have only one engagement and one wedding to plan, could not understand the recurrence of Frances' unfortunate progression of marriage preparations.

"Do you think we should inform Sir Christopher? He is walking in the rear gardens with Mrs. Heffelfinger."

"They shall not be left out of our celebration." Lady Langford backed toward the doors, preparing to quit the room. "I expect he already knows what has happened."

"Kit has known all this time and he has said nothing to us?" Jane said in disbelief. She sounded quite cross.

"I shall have the tea and lemon cake sent in and you can

properly mark this occasion," Lady Langford announced, and with that, she left.

"Clearly you two are perfect for one another. Why did I not think to match the two of you?" Emmeline said, seemingly disappointed in herself.

"Not to worry, Em," Frances assured her. "This happened long before you turned your hand at matchmaking."

fifteen

"THANK YOU FOR MAKING me known to Miss Forbes, Kit." Martin had the pleasure of meeting her at Lord and Lady Raley's ball and thought her quite agreeable. "She is exactly what you have professed. I find her very agreeable indeed."

"Enough to change your mind about matrimony?" Kit's optimism regarding his friend's future went quite beyond the pale. *One* meeting with *one* lady did not alter Martin's outlook on the matter.

"For me?" He smiled, feeling quite certain about his own feelings. He'd learned that marriage was fine for others but not for him. "Not hardly. It would not surprise me to find that I've hardened into a lifelong bachelor but that does not mean I cannot enjoy the company of the fairer sex." That would never change for him. He had hoped he would find someone amiable and settle into a nice family life. Now he was soured on the entire concept. "Which brings me to some news I've heard from Pauline."

"Would it have anything to do with Lady Frances and Albert Winslow?" Of course it would not be news to Kit. Winslow would not even be in Town if it weren't for their mutual friend. To hear him talk he was the one who saved both Albert and Martin from Victoria.

"You have the right of it." Martin's ears were quite worn out. He was happy to attend the ball this evening if only to escape from his sister's continual, bothersome expression of impending bliss the two would experience for the rest of their days upon this Earth.

It was not to be borne.

"Once Albee had decided what he needed to do there was no stopping him from seeking an audience with Lord Langford. He had me take him to his lordship at White's that very evening."

"Did he? Seems a bit rude to disturb Lord Langford's peace and quiet." Martin imagined the earl would not be overly pleased. Until...he realized it was for the more important reason of his daughter's hand in marriage. Martin knew of the urgency. Lady Frances, nor her family, were to blame.

"Needs must, as they say. There was no stopping Albee."

"Can't imagine." Martin shook his head. Still he could not fathom what could drive a man to intrude into an elite club, to which he did not belong. Thus Martin's newly realized belief in his bachelorhood remained firm.

There would be a wife for him...sometime in the future. Perhaps. There was no need for Martin to rush. He wanted a compliant, docile female to ensure a quiet, pleasurable home life. That lady was not Victoria Abbott. However, If Miss Forbes were as agreeable as she seemed, perhaps she might be an acceptable wife for him. It was still too soon to tell.

But a man must marry and Martin understood mutual affection would not take part in his decision. He would not be a participant in what matchmaking mamas termed *a perfect match*.

It seemed to Martin that the ladies had quite another notion about finding a husband and did not approach the marriage arrangement with equal expectations. There was much fuss with gowns, parties, and fripperies.... And they were not above employing all sorts of trickery, deception, and persuasion when it suited them...as he well knew...a list of attributes their potential husbands must possess.

They seemed to flit about and with abandon, spending money, attending parties while gentlemen must earn their regard by a show of affection...or, at least, by the pretense of attention.

"Is this what I have to look forward to when Pauline attends her first Season? Do you think she will be so in love with *being in love* that she loses all good sense?"

"*Wot*?" Kit stared at Martin.

"If that is the typical behavior of young ladies, I wonder if you can expect the same with your Jane? The two seem similar enough, don't you think?"

"*Good God....* I had not even thought of that." Kit blinked. "Is that how females.... No, that can't be."

"I haven't a notion. With my recent experience, I am probably the *last* person you should ask."

"Jane has been quite *transported* with the news of Cousin Frances and Albee's engagement. It has not occurred to me that she...somehow...*imagines* herself in a similar situation. Could it be she is *hopeful* that it might even happen to her soon?"

"I am afraid, my friend" —Martin clapped Kit on the shoulder— "We are wading into uncharted waters here."

Kit babbled something but it was clear he was completely caught unawares.

"At least we are in this together, am I right?"

"*To-gether....*" the baronet repeated, rather absentmindedly and he wore such an odd expression. Martin hoped he hadn't shocked his friend. "Which reminds me— I supposed this may be somewhat related...but I have decided to retain Monsieur Philippe's services. The first lesson is in a few day's time."

"It begins already." Martin felt his resolve strengthened at this news. "I tell you Kit...we must remain vigilant. There is no telling what unsavory character lurks, ready to take advantage of our young sisters."

"Are you speaking of yourself?" Kit shrugged off Martin's arm. "Is that what you have in mind when you approach a lady?"

"Of course not. It's just these...these *ne'er-do-wells*...lack Town Bronze. They have no idea how to behave. Protecting Pauline was not a task I contemplated when we came to Town this year."

"No. It wasn't." Kit cleared his throat. "It was for your wedding and its celebration. How far we have drifted from that path."

Martin had much to regret on that front. "Well, that's what it is, isn't it? I can't imagine Pauline in search of a husband or Pauline *married,* for that matter."

"I suppose it must happen. As it must for Jane." Kit's face blanched. Did he find the thought equally as unpalatable as Martin? "Over there—is that...." Kit pointed to what only one could say was a person illuminated without a source of lighting.

One might have found this unusual. Martin was quite used to the sight of Lady Emmeline. She appeared as no other... always surrounded with some type of *aura.* He wasn't certain if others observed her in this manner, and he did not question the manifestation.

"And is that...."

"Sir Jeremy Hunt with her?" Martin's attention shifted, in its entirety, to Emmeline. "I believe it is...and if I'm not mistaken that is one of her friends but I cannot name her."

"When you discover who she is, I will be obliged to you to

make her known to me. If you will excuse me presently, I fear I need to search for my next dance partner." Kit looked about. "With our discussion, I'm afraid I've lost track of her."

"You'd best be off, then." Martin sent Kit on his way then headed toward Lady Emmeline.

"GOOD EVENING, LADY EMMELINE." MARTIN CHANDLER HAD JUST arrived and made a respectable bow just as Miss Hester Enfield left on the arm of Sir Jeremy Hunt. "I am delighted to see you again."

"Mr. Chandler." Em curtsied. She would never go so far as to admit she was pleased to see this gentleman. That would be an outright lie. If she had set eyes on him first, there would be no meeting now. She had far more important things to do and people to see.

Currently, Em felt quite satisfied for making another successful match between the two parties who departed. Miss Hester Enfield's family were well-off, very successful at raising sheep. Sir Jeremy Hunt's family owned several woolen mills. If their courtship did not work out, it could prove to be a great business opportunity. Either option would benefit their families involved.

"I could not help but notice that you do not occupy the dance floor. That is unusual for you, is it not?"

"I am not dancing this evening," she informed him. Em's reasons were her own business and she need not elaborate. She had much to do this evening than merely enjoy herself. There were matters that required her personal attention. Again, those did not concern him.

"I know there is more than one gentleman who will be

disappointed." He touched the edges of his cravat. It looked to Em that he was nervous. But why? She had never given him a reason to be uneasy.

Martin Chandler was not any of the other gentlemen Em could easily *influence*.

"Perhaps next time." Em felt certain he did not refer to himself and did not regret offering the promise. A closer study of his appearance, beyond his tortured cravat, told her that he had taken some added care dressing for the party. For what exact reason...she had no idea.

Em had to commend him for his simple yet flattering ivory waistcoat. There was a pleasant pastel-colored floral embroidery along the lapels and edges on either side of the buttons, running down the center of his— He must be credited for *not* following Sir Christopher's example by wearing those ghastly waistcoats he had unfortunately made popular, for she had seen others exhibit the very same on a number of occasions. Any mindless creature could display their lack of style and follow that disagreeable trend.

It surprised her that she actually thought of something pleasant regarding the gentleman before her.... It was almost a compliment, *almost*...and she smiled.

Which caused him to smile.

There they stood, smiling at the other.

Em did not understand what had changed between them but their present interaction was a much more favorable effort than earlier in the day when they had come across one another at the Langford residence. There, they could not exchange a single word nor could they remain in the same residence, much less the same room. Now, later that very same day, they were occupied in polite conversation....smiling at one another.

He appeared quite handsome without overshadowing her evening's toilette.

She, on the other hand, contemplated each of her dresses before deciding on which she wore. None of which were plain, ordinary white. That was boring. Em was someone who never thought *adequate* was enough. One ought to test the limits of norm. Thus her gowns were always something a bit more than they appeared on first inspection. A stripe of color, texture, embellishment. Something to make them out of the ordinary and a bit more extraordinary as Emmeline was herself.

Each pleat of Em's small puffed-sleeves, of which there were several, held a secret...a silver-colored ribbon that lay inside and nearly unseen to all. The slight movements she made briefly exposed the hidden ribbon, creating a glint of light, appearing around her shoulders.

And if Em were not mistaken, his gaze drifted toward her arms, thoughtfully examined her sleeves, and skimmed the outline of her shoulders with more interest than he'd ever shown her before.

"If you do not plan to dance, what are your plans for the evening, may I ask?" Martin Chandler sounded more than just inquisitive...he sounded truly interested in what occupied her.

"What do you mean, sir?" Em had just come 'round to changing her perception of him because he might have altered his opinion of her.

"After some moments of observing you...with the other gentlemen—"

"You are *watching* me?" Em gasped in outrage. "How impertinent of you, Mr. Chandler. I am certain there must be some law against such activity."

"I cannot help but feel that you are up to some mischief."

"I realize that you may have had cause to...." After a great deal of reflection, she had decided that it must have been just as painful for him to speak of her impropriety...her indelicate behavior, as it was for her to learn of it. "That was in the past. I want to reassure you that...." She stepped closer, not wishing anyone to overhear, and whispered to him. "I have given a great deal of thought to what you've said to me *that* evening in the conservatory. Upon reflection, I came to understand that" —she did not want to say the words...*he was right*...but.... "What you said had some merit."

"And you have spent your time since then atoning for your many wrong doings?" Martin had clearly seen what she was about. She disliked appearing so obvious. "Instead of making a nuisance of yourself and causing further mischief, you've brought those together who would benefit from an acquaintance."

The compliment made her blush. Unwillingly. Em did not know if he meant it as such but for him to recognize that she had put a great deal of care and thought before making her introductions to certain, chosen couples.

"From what I have seen...have *heard*...you have found great success in your matches." He honestly appeared to be pleased... as if she were trying to *make amends*. "I must commend you on your efforts. It pleases me greatly."

"I believe, Mr. Chandler, you are mistaken if you think I've done any of this for your benefit, far from it. It is only my attempt to set things to right."

A lovely young lady, unknown to Emmeline, extended her closed fan, gaining their attention, and approached.

"I beg your pardon, Mr. Chandler, I hope I am not disturbing you," she said softly. "I hate to be so bold as to seek you out, but our set is about to begin."

"I am sorry I have been derelict in my duty." Martin faced

her, held out his hand to her, and smiled. "I beg your pardon, have you been introduced to Lady Emmeline?"

"No. I do not believe I've had the pleasure." Miss Forbes was of a serious disposition, if the quiet sort was what a gentleman favored.

"Lady Emmeline, this is Miss Forbes." Martin turned and gestured toward his young lady.

"How do you, Miss Forbes?" Emmeline smiled and curtsy to her new acquaintance. Whether they were to become friends...it would have to be seen....

MARTIN LED MISS FORBES TO THE BALLROOM. HE HAD BEEN ON his way to claim his partner for the next dance right after having a few words with Lady Emmeline. He had thought it would take only a few moments of her time. He had no notion they had been speaking for as long as they had, certainly not the entire span between sets. He really needed to be attentive to Miss Forbes, he owed her that much.

They stood across from one another and he returned her smile. She was pretty...beautiful, really. Anyone would think so. Her dark hair, styled in impossible ringlets arranged on either side of her head, contrasted with the handsome white gown she wore, making her appear very regal.

She was wearing *all* white. Only white...and Martin did not wish to admit that it bothered him. One single, solid color with no variations.

The music began and the couples stepped forward and back, beginning the paces of the dance. He moved around Miss Forbes then once again swung forward to stand before her.

Martin wondered what Emmeline was doing since he'd left

her. Was she still standing there alone or would another couple...or gentleman be joining her? He glanced off in that direction to see if he could catch sight of her, see what occupied her.

If he stood very tall, up on his toes to peer over the heads of those that stood between them. He could see a few people keeping her company. Emmeline certainly was not able to hold court as she once had. Her actions from the Blair-Hudson duel must have done her reputation much harm, if Martin were to guess. He recalled when he first saw her how there was a throng around her, vying for her attention—three deep to reach her. She certainly drew a crowd that night.

Martin stepped around and turned with the music and stretched to see the gentleman had approached and was now speaking to her. The man with his arm resting in a sling was easily identifiable as Sir Garrett Hudson who still nursed his injury he had sustained from the duel...over Emmeline, Martin had to remind himself. Yet there he stood, speaking to her amiably...smiling, laughing.

If Sir Garrett could accept her, surely she would once again be welcomed by others in Society.

Emmeline had made it clear she had her own reasons for making amends with others that Martin thought she had wronged. She insisted that *he* had nothing what-so-ever to do with her desire to make amends. She could profess all she wanted...deny that her actions were solely her own...but it could not prevent Martin from having his own opinion on the matter.

sixteen

"I WOULD HAVE THOUGHT Sir Christopher would pay you a call this morning." Emmeline welcomed her friend Lady Amelia later in the week after the Raley Ball. "He seemed quite attentive to you, especially after the last set you shared."

Amelia smiled, clearly smitten by the baronet. She pulled off her gloves, preparing to stay for a bit. It was not as if additional visitors were expected for morning calls were still very thin these days.

"You will be seeing him again, certainly?" Em was glad that her friend had found someone she fancied. It came as no surprise that amiable Sir Christopher was probably more to Amelia's taste than Em's. She may have not thought of putting those two together but it was always possible that she could be wrong.

"He has sent me the most beautiful flowers and he is to take me for a drive in the Park tomorrow afternoon. I am looking forward to it."

Em sent for a tea tray and the two settled on the sofa in the front parlor.

"*Faith*, Em. I grow weary of the Season," Amelia confessed with a great sigh. "The parties seem nearly endless, do they not?"

"You'd best enjoy yourself while you can. Once the Season has finished, parties you tire of now will come to an end. If you should find yourself married by its conclusion, you and *your husband* will remove to your country estate where you may not return to Town until your own daughter reaches the age for her first Season."

"My own daughter? I do not have a daughter.... Em, you put me to the blush. I do not yet have a husband." Amelia covered the heightened color in her cheeks with her hands and stifled a giggle.

"What if Sir Christopher should propose? It is a possibility. Have you considered marrying him? Would you be content? Happy with him?"

"I cannot say that I have truly considered that." By her expression Amelia did not seem overly thrilled by the idea.

"And that is why you need this time...to court him, spend time with him, and make that decision. You do not wish to err in this decision."

"No, I do not. I must agree. It is far too important." She was beginning to see that for herself.

Amelia had the right of it. They were all here to find a husband, make no mistake, even Emmeline needed to...wanted to...not only find a husband but a most agreeable husband. Her once endless choices of *every man in Town* had dwindled and she had not taken her opportunity seriously, playing this time as a game. Enthralling the opposite sex and playing them off one another was not something she should have done. And Martin Chandler's words continued to haunt her—*you must be better than that.*

A footman entered, not with the tea tray but with an envelope.

Emmeline opened the missive and glanced at the sender before returning to the top to read it from the beginning. "It's from Teresa Danvers."

"What does she say?" Amelia peered in its direction, interested, as Em would be, to know its contents.

"She asks that I call as soon as possible."

"You don't think it's happened again do you?" The panic in Amelia's eyes reflected Em's very thoughts. "Hugh Gilbert has not broken with Teresa?"

"Goodness! I sincerely hope not." Em recalled when Lord Hoswell had given Teresa the cut-direct last month and dreaded to think Mr. Gilbert would do the same. For the very same thing to happen again was beyond—

"You should leave now—this very instant," Amelia stood, gathering her skirts, then paused before staring at Emmeline. "Do you think she'll mind if I were to accompany you?"

"I...I think...." If it was true and Teresa needed consoling, two comforting friends would be better than one. "You are a good friend to Teresa—" Em laid her hand upon Amelia's arm— "I'm sure she would be delighted to have you present. Give me a minute to fetch my bonnet, will you?"

CHRISTOPHER STEPPED OUT OF CHESNEY HOUSE ONTO THE WALK and headed toward the street. "If you would be so kind, Mrs. Heffelfinger...." Christopher drew in a deep breath to help clear the cobwebs that had formed in his brain. "You will tell me if I've missed anything, won't you? I believe I might have fallen asleep for a moment...or two more."

"Fallen asleep? Kit, how could you?" Jane wasn't supposed to hear his confession.

"If these *dancing* lessons were to take place at one's own residence, as I believed was to have happened, my presence would not have been necessary." Christopher held the brim of his beaver and wedged the hat onto his head, still feeling unsettled. "My entire morning's routine has been thrown into sixes and sevens."

"To conserve time, and the tedium of the first lessons, Monsieur Philippe's preference is to begin the non-dancing instruction with as many pupils as possible." Mrs. Heffelfinger replied with an exasperated sigh. "Lady Chesney is Monsieur Philippe's patron. She has accorded him with a suite of rooms to conduct his lessons."

"How fortunate for him," Christopher murmured dryly.

"Yes, it is."

"And how *unfortunate* for others of us."

The elder relative proceeded to inform him, "There is a great expense with starting a business and Monsieur has only just arrived from France. You may have found it of some interest had you been paying attention and perhaps a thing or two."

"If I had had a full night's sleep I might have been able to stay awake during the *lecture*." No, he would not have. The dancing master's discourse was remarkably boring. Christopher would even have fallen asleep while standing.

"As Monsieur Philippe's patron, Lady Chesney has him at her beck and call—at any type of gathering, at every party, any time she summons him he must comply." She shrugged and nodded, looking all in all as if that might be a worthwhile arrangement. "I admit, it might prove beneficial for her. Her ladyship does maintain quite an active social life."

"Did you not think of him as *that wretched Frenchman*?"

Christopher clearly recalled that was her response when Jane relayed the tale of the afternoon of their first meeting with the dancing master.

Mrs. Heffelfinger shook off her earlier impression of the foreigner. "That was before I took the time to observe him. The man has such grace and moves with such elegance...if that is a skill he can impart to others.... I have no idea. But if he could...it would be a technique worth acquiring no matter where he is from."

"What good is moving about with your arms wide as if one were thoroughly foxed?"

"Sir Christopher!" she chided.

"I would hardly call it *dancing*...unless one ended up *on* the table, kicking up one's heels."

"Obviously he did not pay attention to a single word from Monsieur Philippe." Pauline, who had emerged from the house, defended him.

"I heard well enough," Christopher replied. "What was the point of taking your shoes off and standing on books" —he gestured with his arms as if to keep his balance— "Carrying cups and saucers on your head.... I thought you were there for a *dancing* lesson. *La pied...sur le livre....*"

"No, it was...*le livre sur la tête*," Jane repeated Monsieur Philippe's instruction.

"*Zee sh-oo-es* must be *aw-ff!*" Is what Christopher remembered and did what he thought was a fair impression.

"We removed our shoes but he did not ask us in that manner," Pauline corrected.

"He does not speak in that manner at all." Jane took great offense at the mimicry. "He speaks without a French accent. He sounds just as if he were one of us."

"And when did you dance?" Christopher returned. "Or had I managed to sleep through that?"

"We did not dance...we were working on our poise and balance...." Pauline took a turn.

"Perhaps this was a colossal mistake to associate with that man in the first place."

The females converged against him—all three of them. They were relentless, berating and censuring him. Mrs. Heffelfinger weighed in by saying, "If you had only paid attention...is that not why you were there in the first place...to look after the girls?"

"Yes, their well-being and happiness are my responsibility and I willingly take it on." Christopher could no longer listen to this schoolgirl sniping and made the decision to bring it to an end. "Shall we visit Gunter's, ladies? I see that you are in need of some ices."

"We did work very hard this afternoon, didn't we, Pauline?" Jane who, to Christopher's knowledge, loved ices above all things.

"Yes, Jane, we did," Pauline agreed.

"Oh, that would be lovely." Mrs. Heffelfinger was never one to refuse a treat.

"I will warn you that there is no place to sit. We shall order our ices and be on our way. Mrs. Chandler is expecting us to bring Miss Chandler home straightaway."

"Yes, Kit. We know," Jane confirmed with the other two nodding in agreement.

"Then let us walk this way." Christopher indicated the direction they should proceed with his cane.

"I know the way!" Jane eagerly took the lead. "I've been there loads of times."

"Many more than what is good for you, I am sure." Her

brother could not blame her for being indulged, he had more than one or two occasions accompanied her there himself.

Mrs. Heffelfinger, happily escorted by Christopher, allowed Jane and Pauline to lead the way. The aunt, whose pace seemed to pick up, also knew the joys of Gunther's. The two young ladies walked together, arm in arm, whispering and giggling in their usual juvenile fashion during the entire journey until they finally rounded the corner to Berkeley Square.

As an attempt to stimulate conversation, Christopher inquired, "What is it today, ladies? Citron? Pear? Mrs. Heffelfinger? Bergamont?"

"And what flavor for you, Sir Christopher?" Pauline tried to tempt him.

"I will not indulge lest I chance damaging my clothing," he replied.

"You're not very adventurous." It was a remark that made him feel a bit older than his one and twenty years.

"No, I suppose I am not." He was unwilling to take risks in several areas of his life, and in some instances he mused it was best to avoid the risk, deeming the reward not worthy.

Watching the young ladies discuss their flavor preferences, Christopher did not think there were any sillier two in the whole of Britain. Did they behave in this manner because they were together and each encouraged the other? He thought they behaved silly last night. Was it possible they were *sillier* this morning? Did the *dancing lesson* have an influence? The fresh air perhaps? He could not say.

It seemed to him, when observing his sister alone, she lacked this ridiculous demeanor. Perhaps next year, when both turned seventeen and might see their first Season there would be a drastic change in them. For there to be such a difference in their maturity from now until then, in the next twelve months, it would be difficult to comprehend. It would be amazing to observe if it chanced to happen.

It was odd to think of Jane courting not as she socialized now but seriously courting with the intention of finding a husband. Christopher would be taking on the *paternal* role in that instance, and the thought of guiding her through this marriage negotiation business was daunting. He had gone through it once before with Victoria and the marriage settlement was not the problem, in that case it was Victoria herself that proved problematic.

However, Sweet Jane was another matter. Christopher's protective feelings were present from her birth and had always been quite strong. Now that she had met Pauline Chandler...the two were peas in a pod. Over the course of months protective feelings for Pauline evolved as well, but not in quite the same manner.

"I cannot wait until we return next year." Pauline stepped onto the pavement outside the shop with her dish of ice in hand. "You will be returning next year, will you not, Sir Christopher? I mean...with Jane. She is to attend her first Season, is she not? We will both be of age and allowed to attend all the parties and balls we cannot this year."

"I'm not sure anything's been decided in that quarter." Jane sounded a bit disheartened and focused on her cold treat. "I am uncertain if Mama will allow me to Come Out. Victoria has yet to marry."

"Oh. I had not thought of that." The news seemed very lowering to Pauline's spirit.

"You haven't thought of that because you do not have an elder sister."

"True." Pauline did not allow the unknown future to dampen her outlook for long. "But this Season is not yet over and it is not too late for Victoria to find a husband which means you *could* be Out by next year. It might happen."

"Yes, I supposed it could." Jane thought this a splendid idea and Christopher did not wish to inform the two how unlikely a subsequent marriage proposal for their elder sister would be. News travelled fast, even from London to Bath. Bad news seemed to travel faster.

"And some of the gentlemen we've met *this* year might return next year as well."

He had no wish to speculate regarding Jane's chances of making a match, or if she would return for her Season next year...it would heavily depend on their sister Victoria's situation.

"Yes, you're right, and by then those young men may wish to marry! They might want to marry us!" Jane proclaimed with so much exuberance that only a young lady, a *silly* young lady, could.

"Not if you maintain your childhood attitudes...." Christopher murmured to himself and sighed. The thought of one of the young upstarts that have recently latched on to their recently acquired circle of friends, namely Nicholas, Lord Epping, Sir John Wanstead, and Henry Newbury were not what Christopher imagined the sort he would want to see marry either of these young ladies.

And was that not why he chose to accompany them? To keep the young bucks away. The thought irked him to no end. If either of these two were to hope to make a decent match they would need to learn some decorum and self-control. They could not remain the exuberant, wild-childs they were now.

They needed help to become well-behaved young ladies. When and how that would happen...he was not at all certain. Perhaps the dancing master would be a good influence on the two, and Christopher would continue their *lessons*. With the passage of time and a little instruction, improvements could be made. In that case, Monsieur Philippe faced a great deal of work.

TERESA DANVERS GREETED EMMELINE AND AMELIA IN THE entrance of her home with a wide smile and good spirits that could not be further from the notion that she had parted with Hugh Gilbert.

"I hope you do not mind that I've brought Lady Amelia with me, she happened to be visiting when your message arrived." Em removed her bonnet and gloves, knowing the three would be occupied for quite a while.

"No, of course not. You are most welcome, Lady Amelia." Teresa gestured that they should follow her. "I think I should send for tea."

"That would be lovely." Amelia tugged at the fingers of her second glove and pulled it off before straightening the ribbons of her bonnet.

"You must see this...both of you." The rising delight in Teresa's voice hasten them forward. "I have never seen anything of its like and— You must see this for yourselves!"

Em exchanged glances with Amelia, both were more than pleased that what they had expected had not come to pass and both excited to discover what had so animated their friend. They followed Teresa into the front parlor where she gestured toward a very large bouquet.

"But I thought you could not bear to have flowers near you?" Em knew this to be true. What made this floral arrangement different?

"These are *paper*...." Teresa told them. "Hugh made them himself...every one of them."

"How beautiful." Em neared the table, becoming aware, as she approached, the lack of floral scent. She had never, ever seen anything like this.

"He made them all. Every leaf, every petal, into an arrangement of flowers."

"It must have taken him hours...days." Amelia stepped back a bit, perhaps to take in the entirety of the bouquet.

The edges of the petals were folded paper in various shades of pinks, whites, and yellow. The narrow stems, the fine arc of the leaves, the curve and shape of the various petals of each flower in the arrangement were intricate.

"They are magnificent." Amelia moved forward, standing next to Em.

"Yes, they are. Hugh...*Mr. Gilbert* completely understands my sensitivity to flowers because of his own sensitivity to grasses." Teresa gasped with emotion. His meaningful gesture had touched her. "He's wonderful, Emmeline. I cannot thank you enough for making him known to me." Teresa went on. "Of course we cannot go for a drive in the Park but we did walk to the lending library."

Of course they did. Em had heard of the tale some days ago. She had hoped they were getting on well but *this...this...*great expenditure of time and effort spoke volumes to Mr. Gilbert's attachment to Teresa could not have been more clear.

"I have never been more taken by a gentleman, Emmeline. He is all that is kind and considerate. He makes me so *very* happy."

Em wasn't certain she should come right out and ask but did anyway. "Are his intentions serious?"

Teresa smiled and blushed. "Yes, I think they are."

"And you are happy about it." Amelia wanted to know but the answer seemed obvious.

"Yes, very." Teresa reached out to Em and took hold of her hand. "I think it's all due to you. If you hadn't introduced us we never would have met."

"You give me too much credit. I am sure that is not true." Em only provided an introduction, she could not have created the affection they shared. "Two suitable people must have found a way to meet."

"I would like to think so. He has asked me to marry him," she confessed. "It's a secret right now. Hugh must speak to Papa first but I'm sure he'll say Yes."

And why wouldn't he? Emmeline smiled. Mr. Gilbert was a most unexceptional gentleman.

Seventeen

An exhausted Mrs. Heffelfinger headed to the kitchen to send in a tea tray for the ladies after seeing Monsieur Philippe and his assistant to the front door of Grayson House after the private dance lesson had concluded.

"I can hardly believe it's been a fortnight since we've begun our lessons." Pauline could not imagine they had spent so long with mere *instruction* and not dancing. Monsieur Philippe said there was a purpose—all the standing about? Did one's *stance* and *bearing* make such a difference? She did not see how it would matter.

"If you can call your aunt and the housemaid *dancing partners*. They were bodies who stood across from us and occasionally lended their hand for us to hold while we *posed* again." Until that happened, Pauline could not muster any excitement for the small progress they made. "I believe that would make a great difference."

"Of course it will. To be honest.... I think I might find it distracting. I do wish to improve." Jane grew very serious then in the next breath wondered, "I wonder if Monsieur Philippe will teach us how to *flirt*—just a little."

"Ahem...." Pauline wasn't certain how to answer. It was not as if Jane's suggestion came as a shock but.... "I do not believe that is...Monsieur Philippe may leave our flirtations to us."

Pauline did not wish to say Sir Christoper's initial assessment was correct but she could not help but think the dancing master was a bit of a bore. While the baronet had previously found it difficult to remain awake, Pauline thought the very same while she stood. The posing and striking attitudes felt as if it would never end, the actual *dancing* portion seemed to be lacking.

They would stand motionless, looking straight ahead, without expression. Monsieur Philippe walked up and down the line of pupils, today it was a line of two, tapping his baton to the beat of the music, touching them lightly to alter the height of one's hand, arm, or lower limb. He never came into physical contact with his pupils. The Monsieur was all about presentation and performance.

The process was tedious and it gave Pauline ample time to glance about. It seemed the dancing master had a keen awareness of when her attention strayed. Perhaps it was a skill learned by trial, mastered by experience. Monsieur Philippe wanted the pupil's full attention on their lesson.

Pauline was not about to waste her time, nor the opportunity to take advantage of his services. As tedious as this was, she had to admit it took great concentration to make her efforts appear natural and easy.

Her arms began to ache as she held them out to her side for what seemed *hours* on end. Moving their position and shifting her weight from one foot to the other—Monsieur Philippe, strolling behind her, tapped her extended foot with his stick, reminding her to point her toe—did little to alleviate her discomfort.

She could not complain. They had desperately wished for dancing lessons, perhaps this was a case of *be careful what you wish for*...because they could not moan that they had gotten their way.

After mastering posture, to Monsieur's satisfaction, they moved on. Jane on one side of the room and Pauline on the other...plenty of space between them...there would be no collisions of the two while they performed, in unison, the actual steps of the dance.

"*Chassé.... Chassé.... Chassé.... Assemblé.*" The dancing master called out in heavily-accented French. Jane and Pauline would point their right foot forward *and* step-together, step-together, step-together, and hop. "And again.... *Chassé.... Chassé.... Chassé.... Assemblé.* And again...."

And again. Would this never end?

Pauline was quite certain this was not the manner in which Martin learned to dance. She was convinced that his instruction was by rote where his dancing master demonstrated the steps and movements and he merely imitated them. It had been sometime since she had seen her brother dance but he could not look as *proficient* as those who learned beside her.

"Ah, me!" Jane flopped into a chair without a trace of refinement, deeming all the grace and elegance she's spent hours practicing during her lesson a complete waste. "Pauline! I can bear it no longer—I am *so* tired!"

The following week, following another such dance lesson, Lord Epping handed his sister up into the Kennington-crested carriage. Immediately after seating herself Emmeline opened her parasol to protect herself from the harshness of the sun. Her brother stepped up after her and settled onto the bench opposite.

He stretched his arms wide, resting them on the back of the seat. "Kennington House, if you please, John."

"Right, your lordship." The coachman released the break and with the call to the horses they were off with the cheerful jingling of the harness and the brisk clopping of the horses' hooves.

"Thank you for including me, Nicky." Em understood why her brother needed to attend but she had not realized how much she would benefit from the lessons. Monsieur Philippe was quite a good instructor and welcomed her as a competent partner for his demonstrations. He did not merely teach dancing which Em found quite refreshing. She found she had, in fact, learned a great deal from him.

"For whatever reason, you seem to have nothing better to do nowadays, dear sister. Have you fallen out of favor?"

"Let's say I prefer to keep my own company for the present—taking some time for a bit of self-reflection, I expect." Em almost regretted spending so much time indoors when it was such a fine day. "Nicky, would you mind if we took the long way home and drove through the Park?"

"You would chance being seen with your *brother*? In such a public place?" By his expression, she could tell she had honestly shocked him, and it made her laugh. That was an occurrence that rarely happened.

Em leaned a bit forward to address Nicky. "I could do far worse than *you*," she teased.

He turned his head toward the coachman and called to him, "My sister would like to drive through the Park, John Groom."

"Very well, my lord." It did not take long to feel the change of direction as the carriage turned and moved in nearly the opposite direction from whence they were originally headed.

"Something about you has changed, Em." He tilted his head back to see her more clearly from under the brim of his beaver.

"In what way?" Em tilted the canopy of her parasol lower to keep the sunlight out of her eyes and off her face.

"I don't know...more kind? More reasonable? And I have to admit, after spending all this time standing across from you... *staring* at you in that manner Monsieur Philippe requires. I have realized that you have an elegance that I admire greatly. You have a presence that is agreeable and very pleasing to the eye."

"*Nicky*—is that a compliment?" Now it was Em's turn to be shocked.

"I am merely pointing out a fact. I believe that elegance and grace come naturally to you. I doubt there are many that will achieve that degree of proficiency, despite Monsieur's guidance."

"Thank you, Nicky." She didn't know what else to say and replied to her brother as she would any other gentleman who praised her.

Their carriage rolled through the gates of Hyde Park. They weren't there at the *fashionable* time where there would be a line of carriages in both directions, the hurry and flurry of conversing with the gentleman near you and conducting discreet social interactions from carriage to carriage as they passed one another.

A few carriages rolled along in the distance but not near enough to disturb the calm surrounding her. Perhaps this more unfashionable, undesirable time suited her. It was pleasant outside, warm with a promise of it growing warmer. All she wanted was to enjoy the sights and sounds of the afternoon.

"*Em-me-line!*" She heard from somewhere in the distance.

There may have been fewer occupants in the Park but they must have been far from being alone.

Both she and Nicky glanced around, trying to discover who dared shout her name in so public an area. It was rather vulgar, really.

"O're there!" John Groom pointed off to the left. Both Em and Nicky focused their attention in that direction.

There was a couple on the footpath not far from them. Em saw a man facing them, waving his hat, as to be noticed. It wasn't so much the brandishing of the beaver that caught her attention but the splash of orange and yellow along his midsection that could have been a beacon in the midst of brown and green of the surrounding trees and vegetation. Em could well-guess who that might be.

"I say, I believe that is Sir Christopher." Nicky could not have sounded more jubilant. He stood while the carriage was still in motion, resting one knee on the bench and steadying himself with one hand to the back of the seat. "*Oi!*" he signaled, lifting his own hat and returning the gesture.

Em could have died from embarrassment! With some silent request, the carriage immediately headed in their direction, there was nothing she could do to prevent it.

"Lord Epping! Lady Emmeline!" Sir Christopher called out and approached.

Em had the feeling her summons, which initially drew their attention, was now only secondary to her brother's presence until she was able to identify Sir Christopher's companion....

"Amelia!" Em was delighted to see her friend, and had completely forgotten her plans for a drive in the Park with the baronet that afternoon.

Amelia playfully slapped her escort on his sleeve. "You were meant to gain Emmeline's attention, not her brother's."

"Of course...but it would have been unseemly to have you shouting across the Park."

"But it is perfectly fine for you to do so?" Amelia apparently found the two men's interaction as distasteful as Em had.

"They are here now...." Sir Christopher made a grand gesture of acceptance and turned to them. "Would you two care to join us?"

"Oh, yes!" Nicky spoke without giving Em a chance to voice an opinion. He hopped down from the carriage, leaving her behind.

"Epping!" Sir Christopher chided, rather sternly, and nodded to the remaining passenger. He moved to the carriage and opened the door at the same time the coachman lowered the steps.

"I beg your pardon, sister." Nicky doffed his hat with one hand and offered the other to help her down. He certainly could learn a thing or two from the baronet.

"*Why—yes, your lordship, let us join Lady Amelia and Sir Christopher,*" Em mocked, hoping that would teach her brother to be inconsiderate of those with him. "*Thank you for asking.*" She snapped her parasol shut, lowered it, and with an unlady-like grip took hold of her brother's proffered hand. "*Rude!*" she whispered to him, just so he would know exactly what she thought of his inconsiderate antics. Stepped onto the ground, she moved to one side, away from Sir Christopher and toward Amelia.

"Shall we continue, ladies?" Sir Christopher motioned that they should lead.

And they did. The men marched out ahead of the ladies. It suited Em just fine for she found them too loud—their voices and their footfalls.

"One would think they were more interested in one another

than us." Amelia looped her arm through Em's and did not look back.

"I know what you mean." Em nor Amelia need to see their escorts to know what occupied them. They heard every enthusiastic word they uttered. "In any case, I am always pleased to see you, Amelia."

"And you as well, Emmeline," Amelia concurred.

"He has out done himself," Nicky gushed. "What a marvelous creation!"

"Lorenzo is quite the genius," Sir Christopher agreed. "Of course he has the skill but what truly makes this unique is the fabric choice—the sharpness of the print, the vibrancy of the colors. I have no idea where he procures such material."

"Not again regarding those *horrid* waistcoats." Amelia, along with nearly every other female known to Em, must have heard, and seen, enough of those ghastly things.

"And why do you wear *that*? Rather plain, ain't it?" As far as Em recalled Nicky wore a perfectly nice ivory-striped crimson waistcoat.

"Pay them no mind, Emmeline." How Amelia could pretend not to hear them? The men were raucous and opinionated on the matter.

"Been to Monsieur Philippe's for a lesson. He's specifically requested that none of the young men sport the...*gilet du soleil*—that's what he calls them."

"Since you have been so successful matchmaking," Amelia put to Em, "I would ask that you find me a nice gentleman who has no interest in *fancy print* waistcoats."

"He says they are distracting...." Nicky went on.

"What does he have against color?" Sir Christopher sounded puzzled. "From what I've seen, the dance master wears very muted tones."

"You know I cannot make a match…. I only provide introductions." Em could never cause two people to fall in love.

"I would dearly wish to meet a young man who would think more about me and than what he wears."

CHRISTOPHER ACCEPTED A GLASS FROM A PASSING FOOTMAN'S TRAY in anticipation of toasting the honored couple at Langford House later that day. This was an occasion to be celebrated—a small get-together to announce the upcoming marriage of his friend Albert Winslow to Lady Frances Abbott.

"After some discussion, we've decided to expand our guest list for our celebration," Lord Langford announced. "Our bride and groom have finally allowed us to make known their engagement now that the first banns have been read over a week ago and the second reading this coming Sunday."

"We're still far from married, Papa." Frances must have found it easier to speak of her past with only a few of her friends.

"We will be, *Fan*," Albee whispered. "It will happen…not soon enough for either of us, but it will happen."

"The final banns and vows to follow, which, I must add, her ladyship promises a splendid wedding breakfast after the ceremony." He stared pointedly at his daughter. "You *will* be married then, my dear, to this very fine fellow," and indicated Albee with a steadfast stare.

"I am sure you cannot blame Frances, your lordship, she has good reason for wishing to bide her time. I do not take offense."

"You are so understanding, Albert," Frances replied, laying her hand upon his arm. "I hope you do not take the delay in our announcement as a slight of any kind. Tonight we have Sir

Christopher and Cousin Jane who are the closest to my dear Albert has to family. They happen to be our family as well which makes our party a very small one, indeed."

"With only the six of us" —Lord Langford gestured to all of them standing comfortably in the room— "I think this hardly qualifies as enough participants for a proper celebration. We need more guests to share in our gaiety, do you not agree?" Lord Langford was interrupted by voices, other visitors who had arrived perhaps.

"Good evening, Lord and Lady Langford." Lady Emmeline was the first to enter the parlor and dipped into a curtsy. "Sir Christopher...Miss Stiles...and, of course, Lady Frances and Mr. Winslow. Congratulations!" She beamed a smile displaying her delight. "Our attendance was supposed to be a surprise!"

"And so it is!" Albee professed.

"Evening, all." Nicholas, Lord Epping stepped into view. Splendidly decked out in a dark blue jacket and white breeches complemented his waistcoat. A smart-looking pattern composed of three different hues of blue in triangular shapes—there was no mistake that this was a Lorenzo original.

"Puffed up like a peacock..." his sister whispered in a condescending tinged tone. The remainder of her comment was muted by new voices and the shuffling of another arrival now stepping into the entrance hall.

Christopher moved to a position where he could see the newcomers and immediately recognized Martin and naturally assumed he would be accompanied by Pauline. It made perfect sense since she was the fourth member of, whom he understood to be, Cousin Francis' close friends. Instead, the female...the young lady, who had her back turned toward the room, could not be she.

Martin, charged with removing her wrap, seemed to move

very slowly...or perhaps it was only Christopher's perception. The stature was all wrong for Pauline. This person's bearing was more sophisticated...self-assured.... Surely, this was must have been Miss Forbes.

"Miss Chandler!" Cousin Frances rushed to her side. "*Pauline*...how lovely you look this evening."

"This is your engagement celebration." Without appearing overly animated at her declaration, as was her normal practice. Her blossom-colored gown set off the slight green color in her eyes. Pauline behaved in a more mature and dignified manner than Christopher had not seen previously. "I wished to make a special effort with my toilette this evening, the invitation said there was to be dancing."

"Yes, it is my understanding Mama has arranged it for us."

"Pauline!" Jane rushed toward the two, greeting them in the same adolescent fervor Christopher knew as customary. "You did not tell me you were invited!"

"It was a secret, Miss Stiles," Emmeline spoke quietly. "Do you not recall me, only now, saying..."

"*Jane*...." Pauline neared to whisper. Christopher doubted those closest could make out what was being said.

"Oh, yes. Yes. Thank you for reminding me." Jane stilled and appeared to be composing herself. She closed her eyes momentarily.

"*You!*" Martin cried out in shock when he saw Emmeline— but then he smiled. "I had no idea you were to attend."

"Yes, Mr. Chandler. I wanted all my very good friends here this evening." Cousin Frances need not justify Emmeline's presence. "I trust there is not an issue attending the same party, is there?"

"No, oh, no. Not at all." Martin had abandoned Pauline.

Christopher could hardly believe his eyes at the speed at which Martin moved to Emmeline's side.

"It is only that...." He paused as if he could hardly believe she now stood before him. "I believe it has been quite some time since we last met."

"It is good to see you as well, Mr. Chandler." Emmeline held her hand out to him, which he accepted.

"It has been quite some time, my lady." Martin bowed.

"Occupied with other pursuits, I'm afraid," Emmeline explained.

"With your absence it is no wonder Society evenings have been dull."

"You are teasing me, Mr. Chandler," Emmeline would not likely believe Martin's amateur attempts, but then, she must have heard all sorts.

"I beg that you ask anyone...these past few weeks have been monotonous indeed."

Christopher noticed Emmeline's hand remained in Martin's all during their conversation. Neither was Martin quick to relinquish it nor was she in any hurry to draw it away. Was he mistaken to think his friend and Miss Forbes were....

"Now that we are all here, I would like to inform everyone as to the events for our unconventional evening." Lord Langford began. "We shall toast our good wishes to Frances and Albert before the young people enjoy their dancing then we shall all sit for supper. I am certain there will be further toasts at that time. After supper, if you young people would like to continue dancing, her ladyship tells me the musicians are at your disposal."

"Does everyone have a glass?" Lady Langford motioned to the footmen to make the rounds with their trays. The guests readied themselves to wish the newly engaged couple well.

"I would like to welcome you all tonight to celebrate the

engagement of my daughter Lady Frances to Albert Winslow." Lord Langford sounded proud and delighted at his announcement. "I have it on very good authority that Mr. Winslow is a most honorable and amiable fellow. He has the highest recommendation by a member of our family. I am sure you all will wish them happy."

The bubbling of good wishes were audible and everyone wanted to drink to the couple.

"I have one other item I would like to address. The advantage of this particular gathering is that there is not a stranger among us. I cannot tell you what a blessing all of you are and have been to our family.... Thank you, friends" —his lordship raised his glass to one side of the table— "Thank you, family" — he raised his glass to the other side of the table— "Please join me in toasting to the love, health, and prosperity of Frances and Albert!"

"To Frances and Albert!" the guests chorused and raised their glasses.

eighteen

AFTER THE TOAST...*TOASTS*...because only one or two were not near enough for the couple, Kit followed up with one of his own, Lord Langford made another, his second and Lady Langford ultimately intervened and insisted the guests progress to the music room where they would have room to dance in comfort and not rattle about in the vastness of the ballroom.

The bride and groom-to-be were obviously paired and declared the head couple. Other than Frances and Albert, the most popular person in attendance must have been Lord Epping, for both Pauline and Jane had an obvious desire to have him as a partner.

"I am not about to dance with my own brother," Emmeline announced.

"Nor will I." Pauline repeated the sentiment, throwing an acrimonious glance toward Martin. "Not when there are other much more desirable gentlemen available."

Martin reacted immediately with the refusal of his sister and held out his hand to Emmeline who, rested her fingertips in his palm, accepting his offer. This only sparked the contest as to who would be first to stand up with Epping.

"I don't see anything wrong with that but if that is the case" —Jane deduced— "I cannot stand up with *my* brother."

"But Sir Christopher is practically infamous!" Pauline tried to convince her friend that *her* brother would be acceptable.

"He is still my brother," Jane maintained, glancing at Epping, knowing that she must win. A smile crept across her lips.

"Oh, very well." Pauline sighed and made the grand sacrifice of trudging to Kit's side. "I suppose that leaves you as my partner, Sir Christopher."

"Never fear, Miss Chandler," Lord Epping whispered as she passed by him. "There will be another dance before the night is out and we shall have our chance to stand up together."

Martin wondered if that gave his sister hope. After all, it was only a dance. He was fairly certain Kit knew enough not to tread on her toes or step on the hem of her dress.

"That is what comes of not wishing to dance with *one's own* brother...one is left to dance with *someone else's* brother," Pauline remarked, rather unkindly.

Kit pasted on a smile. "It is good to know that I am not your *last* choice, Miss Chandler. I can feel at ease that your brother holds that honor."

Martin would not let his friend's barbs wound him this evening. He could not have been more pleased with his partner for this set. With Kit on one side, Martin faced his dance partner Emmeline. His ability to tolerate Emmeline rested entirely upon his own steady foundation with Miss Forbes. That lady was agreeable and possessed every attribute one would want in a suitable wife, making his life easy and comfortable. In her, Martin had found a sensible, reliable female. She need not feel threatened by Emmeline's pretty face and engaging manner.

"I believe I am the only man in London who has not yet danced with you." Martin had yet to behold his partner from toe to head until this moment. Now he saw Emmeline's primrose colored gown with two rounds of white lace embellishment near the hem which he thought very attractive.

"You must be incorrect. You escorted me to the Lady Charlotte Dolan's Ball last month in the absence of Sir Christopher."

"If you will recall," he reminded her. Their mutual aversion was evident then, but now, after some time had lapsed, they managed to tolerate one another quite nicely. "We arrived and departed together but we did nothing else."

"Oh, yes." She smiled and did not seem to mind being corrected by him. No bitter expression, no harsh retort. "I believe you are right. Although I was certain we must have...but perhaps not."

"We have attended many of the same parties but have yet to do the pretty."

There were four couples on the dance floor. Their two lines shifted and they created a square, two couples facing one another. With the small number of guests the dance felt intimate with only eight of them. The music and the dancing began.

Moving to the music was pleasant enough but the oddly striking sight to see—Epping, Jane, Pauline, and Emmeline, moving in unison. Their backs arched with the same curve, they hopped the same distance from the foot and their arms bent in the same angle, moving as if they were performing in a staged ballet, all performed effortlessly and with ease. It appeared all very perfect and pleasing to the eyes.

Is *this* what Jane and Pauline had gained from their dancing lessons? If so, it was apparent that Lord Epping and Lady Emmeline attended as well. Their execution was quite impressive and Monsieur Philippe would have been most proud.

Frances called on Emmeline at Kennington House the next day. Her very good friend's somber mood might have gone unnoticed by the others last night but Frances could tell something was not right. Perhaps she needed a bit of cheering.

"It is very good to see you. How nice of you to call." Emmeline appeared cheerful in her Jonquil-colored morning gown. Frances could help but notice the absence of flowers that once line the walls of the entrance hall and front parlor. Now, very few remained.

"I thought it would be nice to see you again—just the two of us." Frances worked off her gloves and untied the ribbons to her bonnet.

"Yes, of course. Do come into the front parlor and I shall call for some tea."

"Would it be presumptuous to ask if it might be possible to take a turn in your gardens? The day is fine and it would be a waste not to enjoy it." Frances thought the fresh air might do her friend some good as well. "I am still trying to build up my strength."

"That is a splendid idea. I'll ask for a tea tray to be set up outside, shall I?"

"Let us ask Mrs. Saunders and Mrs. Peckover to join us as well," Frances suggested. "The more the merrier!"

"That is famous!" After Emmeline relayed their wishes to the staff, she turned back to Frances. "Shall we be on our way?"

Exiting the back of the house, the mostly blue sky and the few fluffy white clouds that hung above welcomed them. Frances spied the lazy sweet peas in line with the north wall that was covered with ivy of the enclosed garden. Assorted flowering foliage dotted the areas between the rose bushes. Trees provided much needed shade on the south side and a multitude of greenery spread around their feet. A path etched in the lawn meandered about, leading the travelers on a journey toward the far end of the property. A gentle breeze kept the sun from being overly hot and the thought that she needed her bonnet drifted away.

"This is quite refreshing." Emmeline linked arms with Frances and allowed her friend to lead her while she stared off into the clouds.

"We must walk fairly briskly to the farthest point to gain any benefit from this activity, Em."

"Of course." Their pace increased and it seemed to Frances their exertion was more of an effort for Emmeline. Both were out of breath and broke into laughter when they arrived at their destination.

"I wish we could do this more often." Frances thought Emmeline great fun.

"We are in different places, you and I." Both were daughters of earls, both in Town for the Season. Em's, her first and Frances', her second. "You have found Albert and will soon be married."

"I am most fortunate, indeed." Frances wanted to keep running and laughing far beyond the confines of the garden wall. "I must confess, Em, I never thought I could be so happy. You will be soon when you and Mr. Chandler finally realize what is between you."

"What's that?" The smile from Emmeline's face faded and her arm fell away from Frances' when she took a step back to regard her.

"I understand that you are becoming known for the matches you've made these last few weeks. I suppose you cannot see when it happens to yourself." Frances thought them happy and so very comfortable in one another's company, hadn't it been obvious to all? "I saw how the two of you were at the party."

"Martin was merely being civil. He meant nothing more, I assure you. It was only his sister acting a bit churlish...I believe she only wanted to dance with Nicky," Emmeline supplied and took her first step back toward the house.

"I know Mr. Chandler had previously said some harsh things and you took him at his word. He must care a great deal for you."

"How can you say that? He was monstrous." Emmeline looked away. The joy she had felt only moments ago appeared to have vanished with the mention of his name. "I don't even know how I am able to forgive him."

"But you have, have you not?" Frances tried to regain her attention by moving in front of her, but returning to the unpleasantness surrounding him made matters worse. "It must have been difficult for him to speak so forthright, especially when the truth might prove hurtful. Sometimes it is more difficult for the one being honest rather than the one hearing it. I may be wrong but I think he cares for you more than you, or even he, believes."

"Is that how it was with Albert?" Emmeline ventured.

"I did not know I truly cared for him at first. He was a complete stranger." There was much already going on in her life to take notice of him.

But there he was, standing off to the side. Quiet. Attentive. More brave than Frances could ever have imagined.

"But how did you know for certain you cared for him? He saved your life, of course."

"He had but that wasn't what had changed between us."

"He changed? How had he been different after he saved you?"

"I really hadn't thought about it much. All I can say is, he subdued Russell—because he did not wish any harm to come to me...but I think he might have done that for anyone. It's who he is." Frances tried very hard to identify what it was in him she esteemed. "He did not mask from me any unpleasantness and simply was truthful...even when it shone an unpleasant light on himself."

"You did not think him unpleasant in any way, did you?" Emmeline finally met Frances' gaze. "And you admire him for it."

"Love isn't always straightforward and timely," Frances needed to be honest. It was one of life's lessons she had to learn. And it was painful. "Sometimes it is a struggle and takes persistence to get what one wants. Sometimes, one must take risks."

The glance of pure empathy from Emmeline was fleeting. Perhaps she did not wish to believe what Frances was telling her.

"Deny it all you like, Em. You shall see. If he did not care a great deal, I do not believe it would matter to him so much that you should be seen in a favorable light...by everyone." Frances hoped she had given her friend something to think about.

Today Martin assumed the duty of escorting Pauline and Jane with Mrs. Heffelfinger to the dance master at Chesney House. This allowed Kit the freedom to pay calls and take an early drive through the Park if he so chose.

Normally Martin might have spent the time with idle occupation to fill the mindless hours that passed, keeping count of the number of grays or bays passing by the property, inspecting the cleanliness of his fingernails, or to sack his valet for not having the soles of his shoes properly maintained. After observing the dancing at Winslow and Lady Frances' engagement party he found himself more attentive to the lesson.

One might consider Monsieur Philippe's instruction unconventional. One could not dispute his results. Keenly observing his pupils, correcting them, even minutely of positions, the dancing master spent an inordinate amount of time emphasizing posture and attitude. Particularly when it came to positioning the hands, fingers, and feet.

In groups, it was easy to detect the wayward appendages. The constant practice, reinforcing the gestures, making the motions instinctive to the students, while learning a new step or a series of them, performed without thought. As tedious as the exercise might have been, Martin saw the successful results. When the time came to an end, he felt quite fatigued merely watching.

Martin stepped from the front walk on to Arlington Street with the three females and ushered them forward, bringing up the rear. He was more than eager to relinquish his responsibilities and return his charges to their homes. Perhaps they would all settle at the Chandler residence where his mother would serve them tea and ask about their morning.

"Sir Christopher accompanies us to Gunther's after our lesson," Pauline informed her brother. Which was a ploy that was bound to fail since Martin had no desire to start a rivalry between the two.

"The bergamot ice was very nice," Mrs. Heffelfinger added, stepping forward in an effort to keep up with the small group.

"How nice for you, *pet*," Martin mused thoughtfully. "I expect you will look forward to his escort in a few days when you can return."

"*Mar-tin....*" Pauline wailed in a distinctive whine while the two others merely groaned their displeasure.

"I do beg your pardon but I must return you directly, else I will be late for—" He urged them forward. "Do move on."

"Miss Forbes?" Even Jane knew of his business.

"Yes, that's right." He kept them moving forward and pace brisk. "I have no wish to keep her waiting."

"I can hardly wait until I have a young man to take me for a drive in the Park." Jane's longing was palpable.

"We do not have long for our chance, Jane. We will be Out next year and have our pick of young men."

"I hope I have a beau who is as attentive as your brother. I would count myself very lucky indeed."

"I should hope you would fare better." Pauline glanced over her shoulder at her disagreeable sibling. "We may still have a chance to drive through the Park soon, one never knows. With the right companion and the right chaperone...it might be possible."

"Allow me to educate you on this matter, Miss Stiles," Martin began. "It is not so much the *drive* in the Park as the *company* in the Park—*who* accompanies you, for you would not wish to be seen with the wrong kind of person, and *who* you might you see along the way."

Pauline slowed to stroll next to her brother. "Is it serious with Miss Forbes?"

Martin smiled. "I do not wish to speculate but I believe *things* are going well."

nineteen

"HEY—*HEY*!" CHRISTOPHER CAUGHT Martin's shoulder when he nearly passed without recognition. "Where you off to? Honestly, I have the worst luck finding—"

"Sorry, didn't see you." Martin glanced around as if he had lost something...or someone in the crush at the Danvers' rout. This was gathering the very same day after a successful drive in the Park he shared with *Nancy*.

"Looking for anyone in particular?" Christopher wondered if he might be acquainted with that person, or seen *her* earlier.

"Miss Forbes."

"Are you certain she's attending?"

"I brought her myself, her and her chaperone. I was leading the way up the staircase, and when I reached the landing...I turned about and they were not to be seen. I suppose they went right when I went left." Martin gestured and nearly slapped a passerby in the face, catching them on the back. "Oh, I beg your pardon."

"Serves us right for attending one of these dashed crushes!"

"And you? Have you lost your lady as well?"

"Never had one with me. It is my desire to make an acquaintance with an accomplished, agreeable female this evening."

"You're smelling a bit desperate, Kit." You came alone and hoped to attract someone with that" —he pointed at Christopher's midsection— "Are those *tulips*?"

"You know, Martin...I always thought you a discerning sort of fellow."

"I'd like to think I am...but *tulips*...in *those* colors?" Martin's sour expression told of his displeasure.

"They are crocuses, if you must know." Even Christopher thought the pattern of Lorenzo's newest creation might be pushing the boundaries of sophistication. But where better to wear such a daring creation than to a rout?

"What of Lady Amelia? I thought you found her agreeable."

"I believe she does not find me satisfactory company." Christopher did as much preening as space allowed.

"I cannot imagine why," Martin replied, his gaze dropping to his friend's midsection.

"I am trying not to take it personally." Christopher didn't share that the decision was mutual. He simply did not find her agreeable...it was her attitude.

"You are a very fine gentleman. Do you allow her to view those things? She may find them offensive."

Christopher chose to ignore the comment. How could anyone he admired have such a diverse opinion on aesthetics when they concurred on so many other topics? "I should tell you...I have heard some interesting whispers since my arrival."

"Do tell," Martin said with a raise of one brow and leaning in.

Christopher glanced to his right before uttering, "Sir Jeremy Hunt and Miss Enfield...."

"Yes?"

"Announced their engagement last night."

"You don't say?" Martin replied with mild interest.

Christopher shifted his gaze to his left and continued, "Sir Garret Hudson and Miss Carter...."

"Yes?"

"Announced their engagement this very evening." This bit of news Christopher relayed with a bit more importance.

"Really?" Martin did not appear to be much impressed.

"And" —Christopher looked for those around him who might be eavesdropping, and he softened his voice even more— "That quiz of a fellow...you know the one...*Gilbert*."

"Hugh Gilbert?" Martin supplied.

"Yes, that's the one. Just ten minutes ago his engagement to Miss Danvers was announced. They are to marry by Special License tomorrow."

"What?" Martin recoiled in disbelief.

"They plan to be on their way, touring the capital cities of the Continent for an indeterminate amount of time."

"That sounds mad!"

"Their exact plans, as you can imagine, are not quite set," Christopher shrugged. "That is not the most interesting aspect of all those matches."

"It's not?"

"It is said that all these couples were introduced by Lady Emmeline."

"Emmeline?"

"She appeared to have some *magic touch*...." Christopher thought this revelation quite the salacious bit of gossip...perhaps even more so than the announcements themselves.

"Lady Emmeline?" Disbelief dripped off Martin's reply. "That seems very advantageous for you, since you are well known to her." Martin turned to Christopher and with a clap on the

shoulder said, "You are very keen on finding a wife, Kit. Perhaps you can prevail upon her to make one of those introductions for yourself. Now if you will excuse me."

"THIS IS THE ABSOLUTE LAST PLACE I'D EXPECT TO SEE YOU, Frances." Emmeline was happy to see her friend, and her fiancé Albert Winslow, but why they felt they needed to attend was beyond her. "You said nothing this afternoon. This is not the type of party I'd expect you care for—this is an absolute crush!"

"Routs are not usually my choice but...I wish to hear of your recent successes and I know there is no better place to hear the latest whispers."

"Are you telling me you've come to listen to the *on-dit*?" That shocked Em a bit. Frances was not usually one for gossip.

"I suppose you could say that." She blushed and motioned for Mr. Winslow to stay near.

"You have not come alone, have you, Lady Emmeline?" He glanced about appearing a general concern for Em's well-being.

"Oh, no, Mr. Winslow, my mother is about...*someplace*..." Em glanced around thinking she might catch sight of her, making the rounds to greet friends she had not seen for donkey years. "And there is Mrs. Peckover, of course. And Nicky was good enough to provide an escort but left our side once we entered the house. He's off with his own friends, no doubt."

"I thought I might have a look at Mr. Chandler's situation for myself and half expected he might keep you company this evening." Frances' keen study of Em's expression while she responded did not go by unnoticed.

"No, Frances. I'm afraid not."

"From what I could see...you two seemed to be getting on quite well. I thought perhaps...."

Em thought back to that evening...how agreeable he had been...how nicely they had got on.... It was very pleasant and she did enjoy herself. "You were mistaken, I am sure."

"*Mistaken*?" Frances recoiled. "It is plain that you care very much for his good opinion."

"How could you think I cared what he thought of me?" Now it was Em's turn to be astonished. She did not live by how Martin Chandler regarded her.

"I believe you care a great deal...although you may not agree." Frances smiled, and with that smile no one could be angry. "He did say some unkind words to you and you did act upon his words, making great changes in your life. I do not think you would have done so if you cared nothing for him."

Mr. Winslow was drawn to Frances' side and she slipped her hand through his arm.

"Where are you off to?" It vexed Em that her friend would make such impertinent claims then leave her to ponder the words. Frances had always been the kind, rational member of their group. What had happened to her?

Perhaps she was off to find Martin and vex him in the same manner. Did Frances know that Martin was on the very brink of proposing to Miss Forbes?

Em could not keep from remarking, "Is it your turn to play matchmaker?"

Frances turned back and replied, "Hardly—I wouldn't dare." She leaned toward Em and whispered, "I will leave the stratagem up to you."

185

"I THOUGHT I HAD LOST YOU!" MARTIN EXCLAIMED WHEN HE finally recovered Miss Forbes. As it turned out she was on the second floor, occupied by the hostess, Mrs. Danvers, who regaled a group with a description of her daughter's sudden and intense courtship with Mr. Gilbert.

Martin captured her hand and drew it through his arm so they would not find themselves parted a second time.

"How fortunate. It is truly an unusual story." Martin knew more than he wished he did regarding the couple. "I'm certain she will not omit a word."

"I hope not. I am acquainted with Miss Forbes but not with Mr. Gilbert. It sounds as if the two were an unlikely match...*for anyone*...if I am to understand correctly. They started courting and had so much in common...*unusual* matters of mutual concern, it seems. Their differences and incompatibilities to others made them perfect for one another."

It seemed Kit had heard right. If it was to be believed, it was hailed by all to be an inspired match. Mrs. Danvers, who was obligated to host this evening's rout, had a wedding celebration and preparations for her daughter's wedding trip on the following day. If he were truly interested in the reasons why there was the need for haste no doubt it could be easily discovered.

Martin, it seemed, was not that interested in another couple's, or specifically, *that* couple's courting and marriage decisions.

"What were the chances that *those* two would ever find one another?" Miss Forbes was quite animated when speaking about them. "They are so *perfectly* matched."

"Yes," Martin forced a smile and tried to muster some enthusiasm. "Who would have thought?"

"No, I can't say I had." And Miss Forbes continued, "Believe it or not *he* was not at all popular with many members of the *ton*."

"You don't say," Martin remarked, mostly to humor her.

"They are the envy of every lady in attendance." Miss Forbes gave a heartfelt sigh. "The way he looks at her is...and she gazes upon him as if he is...is...."

"Hugh Gilbert is not *that* handsome." Martin hadn't thought so. He did not think any lady would think Gilbert was anymore than *average* in the looks department. She, Miss Danvers, was more beautiful than he was handsome.

"Every lady wishes for what she has...a *Mr. Gilbert*." Miss Forbes tugged on his sleeve. "Oh, there they are now."

Miss Forbes, as well as every female Martin could see, fell silent and gazed at the couple. He noticed an expression he had never seen before come over Miss Forbes.

Good God. Martin saw it plain now. It was illuminating her face, shining in her widening eyes. Miss Forbes was in love with love. Whatever it was that went on between Gilbert and his intended Miss Danvers, Miss Forbes wanted it too. Well...if Martin wanted Miss Forbes for his wife he had better come up to scratch and soon.

He thought her an acceptable young lady and might make him a suitable wife. Martin would speak with her first, then if she is agreeable, he would seek an audience with her father. Perhaps tomorrow during their drive through the Park would be soon enough.

Yes, Martin would take the first steps for matrimony then and Miss Forbes would no longer need to envy Miss Danvers. Martin could become *her* Mr. Gilbert.

twenty

THE FRONT DOOR OF the Chandler residence opened then closed, rather loudly...it caused Pauline to jump while she reclined on the sofa, rattling the pages of the magazine she held.

"I cannot believe it." Martin entered the front parlor and paced to the far end of the room. His mother came down the corridor and followed him in.

"You look a fright, dear, shall I fetch you a sherry?" It was unlike their mother to offer a strong drink during daylight hours but must have felt something about Martin warranted it.

"No, Mother. I'm not upset, it's just—just—" He closed his eyes and took in a deep breath. Deny it all he wanted, Pauline could see that her brother *was* upset. "This is rather unexpected, that's all."

"You're not making any sense, Martin." She set her magazine aside to pay closer attention to him.

"What is it, dear?" Mrs. Chandler gestured to a chair, suggesting that he might sit.

"It's just.... I was completely caught off guard. I had no idea

—never did I imagine that Miss Forbes had any interest in other men."

"What made you think she did not?" Pauline thought her brother must be a complete clodpole. What female would not make the most of her Season and not cast her net as wide as possible.

"I must be completely naive. She had never indicated she was seeing anyone else but me. That's what I liked about her. She was grounded, very steady, not prone to eccentric flights...or so I thought." He shook his head as if clearing the cobwebs in his brain. "Perhaps I am not meant to find a wife."

"I'm sure it is not that difficult. You will make some fortunate lady a wonderful husband." Those were words that only a mother could say. "Did you propose to Miss Forbes and she turned you down? I did not know your interest in her had progressed that far."

Pauline did not think his relationship had.

"How does someone arrange to meet for a drive in the Park one day and the very next afternoon run off and wed someone else?"

"Who wed someone else?" Their mother really did try to understand and Pauline found his words a bit confusing.

"Miss Forbes."

Did her brother say what Pauline thought he said? *Miss Forbes was married?*

"Martin," Mrs. Chandler began, displaying extreme patience. "Will you simply tell us what has happened?"

"Mother," he addressed his parent and Pauline paid close attention as not to miss a single word. "I arrived at the appointed time to collect Miss Forbes for our drive only to be told by Miss Forbes' mother that earlier this morning she had married Lord

Robert Blair by Special License a mere two hours before. The couple left soon after for his property in Sussex."

A cry escaped from the overcome Mrs. Chandler and she reached for the arm of an adjacent chair.

"What?" Pauline was in complete shock. It was no wonder Martin behaved in a mixture of anger and confusion.

"If I were a weaker woman I might have swooned dead away at hearing the news in such a manner." Mrs. Chandler eased herself into the closest chair. "Why did you not tell me more gently?"

"I did try, ma'am." Martin tilted his head back and stared at the ceiling.

Commotion at the front door revealed visitors and, if anyone were to ask Martin, it was an unwelcome intrusion at an unfortunate time.

"Lord Epping and Lady Emmeline Cordia-Darling, to see the family," the butler announced. "If they are In."

"Of course we are In," Martin replied, his tone impatient. He clambered to his feet, standing when the brother and sister duo crossed the entrance hall, entering the parlor.

"Lady Emmeline!" Pauline set her magazine aside to welcome them and smiled. "*Lord Epping.*"

The purpose for her visit was threefold. One...to lend respectability to the afternoon's outing on Pauline's behalf. Two...the role of chaperone could have been left to Mrs. Chandler or Mrs. Peckover, but Em wished to attend and enjoy the scenery of the Park as she had previously.

It was true that Miss Chandler was not yet Out, and it was true that outings in the Park may not be exactly an acceptable activity, but no one could argue the meeting of family friends and enjoying a drive together.

"Do fetch your bonnet and Spencer, will you? Do not keep

them waiting." Mrs. Chandler motioned to her daughter who immediately complied and quit the parlor. "It is kind of you to ask Pauline to join you this afternoon, Lady Emmeline."

"It is my pleasure, Mrs. Chandler." Em did so enjoy the company of both the young ladies. "I had hoped Miss Stiles might also join us but she, unfortunately, had previous plans."

And *Three*...getting back to the reasons Em wished to accompany the young couple...the truth of the matter was, she wished to be in attendance at the Chandler residence at this particular time to watch...to *see* with her own eyes what had transpired after...after....

Martin sank into the chair behind him, leaning back and crossed his legs. Em thought he gripped the arms rather tightly, most uncomfortably. It was merely a personal observation.

Pauline stopped when she reached the doorway, before departing, she turned, and announced to all and sundry, "We have just discovered that Martin's Miss Forbes has just wed and fled this morning."

There was a strained moment of silence. Both Martin and Mrs. Chandler looked daggers at her.

"Yes, I know," Emmeline replied in complete calm.

"How could you possibly know about this?" Martin addressed her with a slight tilt of his head. "It only happened a few hours ago."

"Because I introduced her to Lord Robert Blair."

"You—" Martin straightened, sitting upright in the chair, and stared hard at her. "You mean to tell me *you*—"

End of Book 2

Grace, Lady Yardley
Marriages

1 Squire John Swithins

Henry Swithins

2 Anthony Pomeroy

Samuel Pomeroy

William Pomeroy

3 Sir George Glory

Sir Christopher Glory

4 Right Hon John Abbott

Victoria Abbott

John Abbott
(heir presumptive
Earl of Langford)

**5 Robert Stiles
Viscount Wyman**

The Hon Jane Stiles

Robert Stiles
Viscount Wyman

6 The Hon Samuel Everett

Simon Everett

Edward Everett

**7 Edward Clifton
Earl of Barlow**

William Clifton
Earl of Barlow

The Hon Frederick
Clifton

**8 The Lord Robert
Beeson**

Stephen Beeson

Peter Beeson

**9 Andrew Tuttle
Marquis of Worsham**

Anthony Tuttle
Marquis of Worsham

The Lord James Tuttle

**10 The Lord Yardley
Grayson**

Hilary Grayson

Richard Grayson

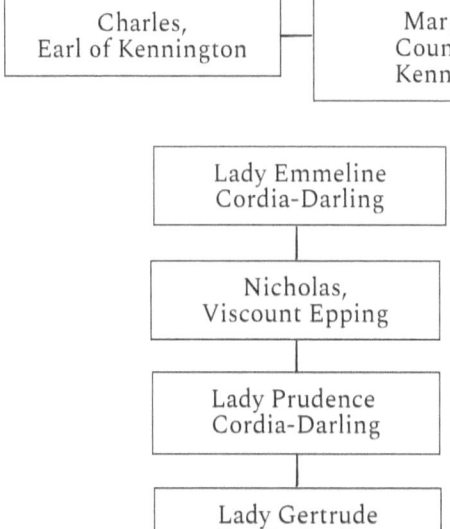

Cordia-Darling Family Tree (Earl of Kennington)

Charles, Earl of Kennington — Margaret, Countess of Kennington

Lady Emmeline Cordia-Darling

Nicholas, Viscount Epping

Lady Prudence Cordia-Darling

Lady Gertrude Cordia-Darling

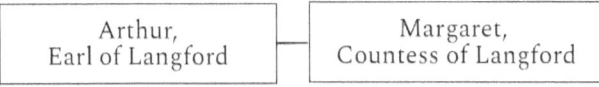

**Abbott Family Tree
(Earl of Langford)**

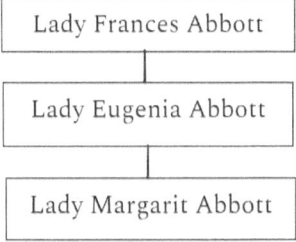

| Arthur,
Earl of Langford | Margaret,
Countess of Langford |

Lady Frances Abbott

Lady Eugenia Abbott

Lady Margarit Abbott

about the author

California-born Shirley Marks lives in Silicon Valley with her software engineer husband and unpredictable Australian Cattle Dog mix. Shirley dreams of returning to London, Paris, and Florence to research settings, develop new characters, and stories to weave together for her upcoming novel. When at home, she spends time reading, writing, and trying to get the odd knitting project completed.

Shirley writes Traditional Regency Romance stories (sweet/clean), clean Romantic Comedies, and a couple of paranormal novels.

You can visit Shirley at: www.ShirleyMarks.com